ROYAL PLAYBOY

NANA MALONE

COPYRIGHT

This is a work of fiction. Names, characters, places, and incidents either are the product of the author's imagination or are used fictitiously, and any resemblance to actual persons living or dead, business establishments, events, or locales, is entirely coincidental.

Royal Playboy

COPYRIGHT © 2019 by Nana Malone

Cover Art by Staci Hart

Edited by Angie Ramey and Michele Ficht

Published in the United States of America

PROLOGUE

XANDER

Present Day

Glass.

Blood.

Some other wet, sticky substance I couldn't identify. But they were all part of my visual field now. As was the smoke.

A roaring in my head was the only sound I was aware of in the chaos. Ignoring the pain in my neck, I reached for my reason for living. "Imani." My voice was more of a growl than anything else, and I could barely get the words out. Trying again, I croaked out, "Imani."

I reached for her, but instead of reaching for me and grasping my hand, her palm was lifeless and cool to the touch. I forced myself to turn a little more, swallowing the pain. "Imani, wake up. Love. Jesus Christ! Oh my God! *Please. Please. Please.* Wake up. Please, God."

I yanked on my seat belt. Why couldn't I move?

I mentally cataloged the aches and pains, assessing my injuries. Everything hurt. I was sore in places I didn't even know I could be sore in. But my concern was not for myself; it was for Imani, my fucking wife. And Jesus, *the baby.*

Someone had done this to her. She wasn't moving. "Sweetheart. Please, God. Please, wake up. Wake up."

And then the deafening silence around us began to dissipate. Slowly. One sound, then another. I heard the shouts. The screams. The sirens. I heard myself. My voice getting traction now. "Wake up, Imani!"

I squeezed her palm, but she didn't squeeze back. My fingers turned to find her wrist, pressing to locate her pulse. I did the one thing I hadn't done in a very, very long time.

I prayed.

I squeezed my eyes shut and I spoke to God. Buddha. Anyone I thought might listen. *Take me. Take me! Not her. She does not deserve to die.*

If anyone deserved to die, it was me. I was an arrogant, selfish prick. I didn't deserve her, nor did I deserve to live. *God, please take me.*

I felt the faint *thud, thud* at my fingertips, and I was

thankful. But something didn't feel right. Her pulse should be stronger than that, shouldn't it?

There was someone at my door. Security maybe? They'd been in the follow car. I shook my head, directing him to the other side. "No, her side. She's unconscious. Help her."

But they weren't listening. They were opening my door, and hands were reaching in.

I shook my head. "No, help her."

Still, they didn't listen, and a hand reached for me. I tried to fight them, but I couldn't fucking move.

The next thing I knew, somebody was cutting off my seatbelt and they were pulling at me. I tried to fight them off, but I was sluggish, uncoordinated. Fuck, what was wrong?

Then I saw people at her door, opening it, pulling her to safety at last.

They were helping her. Oh, thank God. Please, please. She was all I had. She and the baby were the only things grounding me. She couldn't die. I wouldn't let her die.

Then they were putting me on something hard, unmoving. A stretcher? I was fine. Everything hurt, but I was fine. They needed to help her. I tried to roll over, but someone put his hand over my shoulder. "Oi, mate. Lie still. We're trying to save you."

I shook my head, trying to remove the mask he was placing on my face. "No. Don't save *me*. Save *her*."

3

His face was stern as he frowned, but his voice was gentle. "We are saving her. You'd be no good to her dead. So lie still and let me get the oxygen on you."

My gaze swung to her. "Please. She's all I have."

She was the love of my life, and I hadn't taken care of her.

I had done this. My hubris was the reason she was here. From the moment I'd met her, I'd put her on this collision course. This was my fault. If she died, I was one hundred percent responsible. And I was never, *ever* going to forgive myself.

※ ♣

Xander

One week.

One solid week, I'd sat in this chair.

A solid week I'd spent holding my wife's hand, insisting that if they were going to treat me in any way, they had to treat me right next to her. I wasn't willing to be away from her.

It was one of those times I'd pulled every string I could. Because there was no way in hell I would leave her.

I'd emerged from the accident surprisingly well.

Despite a broken left wrist and a fractured collar-bone, I was mostly fine.

Imani had several broken ribs and some internal

injuries, including a ruptured spleen. Our daughter, surprisingly, was unscathed. Her heartbeat was still strong, and she was fighting.

Imani's last surgery had been that morning and the doctors said she should wake up any moment, but still, she wasn't up. Her dark eyes weren't rolling at me. I hadn't seen her smile in three days. *Three* days since I'd made a decision that would forever impact us. I had messed up.

You can fix it.

And I was going to fix it.

There was a knock at her door, and I called out, "Come in."

"Mate, it's good to see you up and about."

I nodded at my brother. "Hey, Lex."

"How is she today?"

I shook my head. "More of the same, I guess."

"What did the doctors say?"

"Just that she should be awake. But she's not."

Wake up my love. I'm a selfish bastard, and I need you. I kept talking to her because I heard somewhere that you're supposed to talk to people in a coma. So I continued to verbally walk her through our everyday lives. And it wasn't full of roses, but it was full of love. I talked so our daughter could hear my voice and know I was waiting for her, that I wanted her to keep fighting.

I talked to keep myself from going crazy.

Lex deposited the flowers he'd brought for her into a

vase, simultaneously scooping out the wilted ones from a couple of days ago and tossing them in the garbage. "Look, you know how strong she is. She's going to get better. You've got to believe that."

"Oh, I believe it. In the meantime, I need to *do* something."

My brother narrowed his gaze at me. "Xan, I know that look. You and I both know that look does not lead to happiness."

"What look?"

"You know, the look of hatred and revenge. We've been down this path before."

"Yeah, and it worked. He got what was coming to him."

"Yeah, but at what cost, Xan? You? You can't do that shit anymore. A week ago, you were ready to sign on to be Mom's successor. This isn't you."

"It's absolutely me. What? Just because I fell in love, you think I've been tamed? Nope. I'm still a prick. A prick who, when fucked with, will fight to protect his own."

Lex leaned against the wall. "I hear you. Do you think I don't want to protect her? She's my family too, Xan."

I worked my jaw. I wanted to lash out at him and tell him that Imani wasn't his family, she was *mine*. Mine to protect. But I knew what he meant. And it was true. My wife was his family, and his wife was mine. We'd all walked through the fire together.

We'd survived the skeletons of our past and those that

threatened our futures. We'd been through a lot together, the four of us, so she was his family. But she was still *my* responsibility. "Lex, you don't want any of this. Whatever I do, it's going to be ugly, and you need to protect Abbie from it. I'm planning on making this right."

He shook his head. "Xander, you need to listen to me. I know this hurts. I know that you want revenge on the person who hurt her. I want that too, but revenge is not justice. What you're thinking... I can see it on your face. We've already been down this path. It turns you into someone you're not."

"And who said that I'm not that person?"

Fury simmered just under my skin. A long time ago, I had one hundred percent been this person.

But then you found her. And she made you a better person.

She did make me better. But now she was lying in a fucking hospital bed and wouldn't goddamn wake up no matter what I said. No matter how much I prayed. Begged. Pleaded. She wouldn't fucking wake up because someone had done this to her. So as far as I was concerned, that someone was going to pay with their life. I met my brother's silvery slate-colored gaze, so like my own, And his eyes were narrowed in concern. "Lex, I need to do this. If this had happened to Abbie, you'd do the same thing."

I waited for him to try and deny it, to try and tell me that he wouldn't go down this path, but I knew my brother.

When the chips were down, he would do whatever it took to protect his family, just like I would.

I took Imani's hand and pressed it in mine. She'd always had the worst circulation. Her fingertips were cold as I leaned forward and kissed her knuckles. "It's okay, angel. You rest. You wake up when you're ready. No matter what, I'll be here. In the meantime, while you get some rest, I'm going to deal with the people that did this to us. No one is ever going to hurt you again."

That sounds like a familiar promise.

Four years ago when I met her, I was a completely different person. One who believed in doing whatever I had to do to get the job done. And now I had to channel that person. But I'd had so much love in the last four years, gone through so many changes, I wasn't sure if I could.

Well, you'd better figure out a way, because if you don't, they're going to get away with this.

Lex cleared his throat. "Do you want me to sit with her for a while?"

I shook my head. "No, you go home to Abbie. I'm just going to sit here and talk to her a little longer.

He nodded and gave me a faint smile. "Are you going to tell her the story of how you met again?"

"You know what? It's not a bad idea. Maybe that's what she needs to hear to wake up. In the meantime, can you make some calls for me?"

He sighed and nodded. "It's already done, Xander."

I met his gaze and lifted a brow. "So, all that talk about not getting revenge was bullshit?"

He shrugged. "Well, I was hoping to talk you out of it, but I know you too well. And if it was me, I'd want the same thing. I'll let you know what I hear. In the meantime, you tell Imani the story of how you met. Let's guarantee to wake her up so she can slap you."

I chuckled softly. "Yeah, you probably have a point there."

At least I hoped he did. I would do absolutely anything to get back the woman I loved.

CHAPTER ONE

XANDER

Four Years Ago...

Pussy came easy. But then, for me, most things came easy.

As I slid a glance over the lithe, naked back of the blonde in front of me and locked my teeth, I wished some things came easier than others. It didn't matter how much my balls ached or how much sweat dripped off my brow, there'd be no relief for me, no matter how many times I had her.

As she moaned, writhed, and shouted things that were dirty enough to make any porn star blush, I fought to stay focused. She was a means to an end. Unfortunately for me, that end wasn't pleasure. It was more like revenge. She had information I needed. And she, like half the women in London, was susceptible to the Chase charm.

She screamed through her orgasm, and I just wanted it to be over. *A means to an end.* She was Alistair's wife. Screwing her was one more domino on my way to taking down the man I hated.

My brain did me the favor of replaying the night over and over and over again. Every decision I'd made. Every step that had led me there. How well she'd sucked my cock on the way to Notting Hill. The slide of her tongue over the length of me as I spun my Huayra over the rain-slicked streets of London. The feel of her pussy milking my cock. Her brazen offer for me to have her any way I wanted.

But I had zero desire to come. And no amount of fucking this nearly nameless, faceless blonde would solve that. After it was over, I'd barely remember her. Hell, I could barely remember her name as it was. Georgina? Jemima? Julia? Something J-sounding. Bugger, I really did have to get better with names. But I *would* remember whose wife she was.

I pulled away from her, and she made a half-hearted, feeble attempt to reach for me. Who was she kidding? That was orgasm number four for her. She'd be out cold in seconds.

I slid the satin sheet over her naked form and sat on the edge of the bed. My dick twitched as if to remind me of how I got into this mess in the first place. I scrubbed a hand down my face. I sat there for several minutes until her deep, even breathing alerted me to her slumber. *Right. Time to go to work.* I tugged on my boxer briefs and slipped into the living room where she'd dropped her bag.

I made sure I kept an eye on the bedroom door as I booted up her laptop. Thanks to one tequila too many and my very skilled hands working their magic under her panties, she'd told me everything I needed to know to take a decent stab at her password. I got it on the third try. *Cat's name.* I didn't bother to roll my eyes.

When I was done copying all the files to my external hard drive, I shut down her computer and slid it back into her bag before silently stalking back into the bedroom. She was still knocked out, but the sheet had shifted slightly, exposing her bare arse. *Fuck.* Maybe I should have taken her up on her offer to fuck her however I wanted.

I scowled at my straining erection. My cock begged me to go back to bed. To give it another go in the hopes that this time would be different. That *she* would be different. But I knew better. What was the definition of insanity again? *No point in going back to it, mate, it won't do any good.*

There was only one way to relieve the gnawing, clawing hunger. But knowing the solution didn't mean I wanted to go through with it. *Get in the shower. Release the tension. Then call the cleaning crew to deal with the unwanted guest.* Most importantly, I had to ignore that niggling thought at the back of my skull. That tiny voice telling me the kind of man I was. Telling me that inside, I was beyond buggered. Truly fucked up and there'd be no respite for me. This was my personal hell.

I didn't bother to tiptoe into the spacious bathroom because I knew she wouldn't wake up anytime soon. I avoided the mirror and stepped into the shower, blasting on the hot water and letting the piercing pellets from multiple sprays scorch my skin. In a long-practiced move, I reached for the shower gel, using just enough to coat my hands, then I stroked myself.

A harsh groan tore from my throat on contact. So, bleeding good. I focused on the memories of the woman in my bed. The gentle, yet suggestive smile as she'd brushed up against me. That was always my favorite part. The possibility of something great.

Of course, it was never great. At that point, I doubted I'd know an epic shag if it came up and bit me on the arse. But I kept repeating the same patterns over and over again. What was the definition of insanity again?

It didn't help that, thanks to the Chase name, the royal connections, and my face, woman after woman happily climbed into my bed.

But the end result was always the same. I was dead inside. My balls ached as I stroked myself, my palm smoothing over the flared tip. I hissed in a pleasurable pain at the friction. So... on edge... almost... Just needed...

My release hit me with the force of a tank, and I shook violently as stream after stream of come shot out of me. I clamped my jaw tight, unwilling to cry out with my release.

As soon as it was over, I did what I always did and turned the water as cold as I could stand it. Then I let my body slide down to the tiled bench seat as the self-loathing seeped into my pores.

There had to be a better way. I would only survive so much more before I became irrevocably broken. Maybe it was already too late for that.

⚜

Xander

My heart thundered with each step, and I fought to control my labored breathing. The more I pushed, the more everything burned. My lungs, my chest, the muscles in my thighs, my overly taut calf muscles. In contrast next to me, my brother seemed completely unbothered as we pushed the pace of our run.

With the spirit of competition riding me, but more the need to outrun my demons, I pushed harder, forcing my legs to move faster. Next to me, Lex matched my pace but his breathing hitched, and I smirked. The way I saw it, we both had some demons to outrun.

Despite my hoodie, the chill of the morning settled into

my bones. Or maybe that was still the slithering stench of self-loathing. I'd left the J-blonde in my bed. If she was still there, the cleaning crew would arrive soon enough to help her along her way. And even if she tried to wait for me, she'd soon realize I wasn't coming back. Not anytime soon anyway. I didn't live there.

That flat was strictly for sex and for women I had no intention of ever seeing again. There was no way I was bringing anybody to where I actually lived. I didn't need this feeling permeating into my real life. *It's already here.* Separation of fucking and life was important to me, and never the twain shall meet.

I had far too much riding on my goals. It was time I got serious. I couldn't afford to get distracted. At least that's what I told myself as I forced my legs to keep going.

Out of the corner of my eye, I saw a woman bundled against the chill of the morning pushing a baby pram while she jogged. Her chocolaty complexion reminded me of the one woman I shouldn't want and couldn't have. Instinctively I turned to get a better look.

That brief break in concentration tripped me up. Literally. I went arse over teakettle on the grassy trail, forcing Lex to jump out of the way.

Through labored breathing, my brother leaned down and offered a hand. "All right, Xan?"

I glared up at the hand offered and scowled. I wanted to take it, I really did, but I'd punished my body and the prone position was feeling far too comfortable at the moment. I didn't stand. "Fine."

Lex dropped smoothly to his side in the dewy grass. "Glad to hear it. Now maybe you can tell me why we're running like we're in Olympic training."

"What's the matter, my pace too fast for you?" I deflected immediately. Lex was too adept at seeing through me. We'd been through too much together.

"I kept up, didn't I?" With a sigh, Lex tried a different tactic. "What's really going on with you?"

"Sorry. My mind's just on the purchase of Trident Media stock. I need everything to go right. It's got me edgy."

Lex nodded and ran a hand through his dark hair. "I understand. Though, if it's causing this level of stress, maybe we shouldn't be doing this."

I watched my brother from the corner of my eye. There was no mistaking we were brothers from our tall, lean frames to our facial features, our coloring, and our silvery-gray eyes. Only Lex's hair was inky and dark, while I still sported the dirty-blond hair I'd had as a child. But some days our personalities were so far on opposite ends of the scale I wondered how we could be brothers. "Didn't we already cover this territory?" For months, since I had told him the plan, Lex had tried to talk me out of it. "You don't think that fucking twat deserves to pay for what he did?"

"Of course I do. You *know* what happened on those

stairs that night. But this plan of yours, it's eating at you, Xan. Corroding you from the inside. You've been edgy and snappish, even to Abbie, who you normally think walks on water."

I winced at the mention of her name. Abbie Nartey shouldn't have meant anything to me, considering she was my brother's girlfriend. But from the moment she'd become my student, I'd had a soft spot for her. *Make that a very hard—never mind.* She was the reason my brother smiled again. And she was my student. I'd put aside the feelings I had for her a long time ago. *Mostly.*

"I'm not exactly the warm, soothing, agony aunt. She knew that about me when she took the job." And normally, she gave as good as she got. But Lex was right. Even I knew my mood swings were a special kind of toxic.

"This is what I want, Lex. I *need* to do this. Then I can walk away. Start fresh. I can't let him walk around like he owes us nothing. He could have stopped the abuse at any time, but he didn't. He could have told someone, but he didn't. And he could have admitted the truth, but he didn't." What I didn't say out loud to my brother was the secret shame I carried. *He didn't have to hold me down for his father, but he did.*

No. We'd continue with the plan. Alistair McMahon's company, Trident Media Group had been financially back-sliding for some time, and they'd been selling off chunks of stock to recoup their losses. Stock Lex and I had been purchasing through various companies. For now, we were holding on to it, but when all our ducks were lined up in a row, the two of us would have enough shares to dismantle Trident brick by bloody brick. And thanks to the information from J-girl's laptop, I might have something big enough to destroy him for good. "I have the information we talked about."

Lex shook his head. "Do I even want to know how you got it?"

"Nope."

"Xan, this is a dangerous game."

"Go on with the stock purchase. I've got Garett working on the data. If there's anything on her computer we can use, I'll let you know. In the meantime, I'll work on phase two."

Phase two was more difficult. Alistair McMahon sat on the board of London's Artistic Trust. I had to get myself on that board in order to topple all of my dominos for a more effective blow. But getting on the board was easier said than done.

My brother studied me as if he could divine the truth out of me, then eventually sighed. "Okay. Do you want to continue this grueling pace, or have you had enough?"

I pushed myself to a standing position. "We can take it easy heading back."

Lex smirked and bounced up next to me. I wanted to curse my brother's energy. My legs felt like lead weights.

That's what happens when you try to outrun demons. "Who said I needed to take it easy?"

"Of course, you don't."

I tried to stand, but I groaned instead. "On second thought, I still have some kinks to work out."

"I'm proposing to Abbie." It was blurted out in a rush, and Lex flushed red as he said it.

For several long moments, I couldn't compute the pain that radiated through my chest or the words that caused the piercing headache in my skull. But slowly, the words started to piece together. *Propose. Abbie.*

That was it. In that moment, I knew what I had to do. I'd shut the door ages ago on anything ever happening with Abbie, but a piece of me hadn't let her go. Though it was less about her and more about what she represented. But she was all Lex's now.

The guilt was quickly overshadowed by joy. I might be in excruciating, radiating pain, but Lex looked happy. The kind of happy that people could only experience when they had nothing holding them back.

I let that joy from my brother fill me and drown out the guilt and the remnants of pain. Pulling my brother to me, I hugged Lex hard. While I embraced him, I blinked away the stinging in my eyes. I could be happy for him. If anyone deserved that kind of happiness, it was my brother. And Abbie of course. Especially since Jean Claude had threatened to kill them both. I could have lost them. This, this was far better.

There was no point in feeling any loss for myself. It wasn't my moment. "Mate, I'm so happy for you." Lex hugged me back, and we stood there in the middle of the park embracing each other. When we pulled back, we both ignored each other's misty gazes.

Fuck, why couldn't I rid myself of the impending tears? "Good for you. Now you tell Nick that he may be your best mate and all, but I'm the one standing next to you on the big day."

Lex used his t-shirt to wipe his face. "Well, let's get her to say yes first, shall we?"

"Let's face it, she's nutters about you. She'll say yes." And somehow, I'd have to figure out how to deal with that.

My brother licked his lips. "You're okay, though?"

"I'm bloody brilliant. I'm about to get a sister."

CHAPTER TWO

IMANI

I hustled along Savoy Way, clutching my bag to my side, desperately trying to fit my whole body under the minuscule umbrella.

That was what I got for forgetting mine at home and having to grab one from the corner shop. The number one rule of living in London was *always bring a freaking umbrella*.

Tilting my head back, I tried to determine how much farther I had to go to reach the Savoy. Of course, the moment I did, rain pelted my face with sharp, stinging pellets.

Up ahead I saw the marquee above the Savoy, and I breathed a sigh of relief. Once inside the foyer, I shook out my umbrella and tried to psych myself up for the appointment my director had set up for me.

Since I would be playing the lead in the play adaptation of the hottest book to hit Britain since *White Teeth*, he thought it would be a good idea for me to do some research. In this particular case, since my character was a prostitute, I was on my way to meet an escort.

When I was accepted into the acting program at the Royal Academy of Dramatic Arts, I couldn't believe it. Each year they only accepted twenty-six students. It was practically unheard of for them to take an American, but they had. And I'd made the painful choice to escape. But I'd left a piece of myself behind back in New York.

The hostess directed me to a secluded booth near the back where a pretty brunette sat sipping champagne. She stood smoothly as I approached. "You must be Imani. I'm Miriam." She shook my hand and kissed both my cheeks. "It's a pleasure to meet you. I must tell you, most actors I encounter are pretenders, so full of themselves. It's a pleasure to meet the real deal."

I had no idea what I had been expecting, but this pretty, cultured girl wasn't it. In the light, her skin was more café au lait. And her eyes were a lovely chocolaty brown. With her hair up in an artful messy side bun, she looked chic. Not exactly what I had expected from an escort. "It's uh, nice to meet you, too."

"You seem nervous."

"Well, you could say that. On the one hand, I haven't

got a clue what to say to you. On the other, I have a million questions."

Miriam smiled at me. "Okay, well, why don't you tell me about your character?"

That was easy enough. *Carmen Jacoby* was one of the hottest plays around right now. When Shane McQueen wrote it, several theaters fought for the rights to the first production. RADA had won out for our senior showcase piece. If we did a good job, it was likely many of the actors would go on to perform it on the West End. It still hadn't sunk in that I'd won the part.

"Carmen is a complicated girl. She's strong and smart, and she sees her body as a means to an end, but not *the* end. She has other dreams. She's a fighter and a bit of a hustler, so she takes advantage of the opportunities presented to her and goes from being a prostitute to a madame, to becoming one of the most successful traders in the city. But through it all, what she really wants is love from the one man she can't have."

Miriam sat back. "And a little slip like you won the role of Carmen."

I jutted my chin out. "Winning had nothing to do with it. I busted my ass the hardest for that role."

Miriam studied me. "I believe it. Why don't you start at the beginning with your most basic question?"

Right. Most basic question. I waited until our cocktail

waitress had taken our drink orders and departed before I delved right in.

"Exactly how did you become a sex worker?" This was a conversation I never thought I'd be having in my lifetime.

The pretty brunette leaned forward and grinned. "What did you call me?"

I shifted uncomfortably. "Uh, a sex worker."

"Love, I'm an escort. A hooker, a slag, a slut, a tramp. A whore. I'm not picky about what you call me. At the end of the day, I have sex for money. *A lot* of money."

Okay then. Rivulets of sweat rolled down my back. It wasn't warm in the bar of the Savoy, but this was a conversation I was unprepared to have. I cleared my throat. "Okay then, when did you become an escort and why?"

Miriam waved her hand dismissively. "I don't have some sad story or anything like that. My old man didn't abuse me. I didn't get into this because I'm hooked on drugs. The truth is I like sex."

I frowned. "You're clearly a beautiful girl. You could have had the sex without getting paid for it."

Miriam grinned. "Then, my love, I would be a very *stupid* girl. So many women are stuck in relationships they don't want with nothing to show for it at the end. At least I have money and the occasional orgasm."

The girl had a point. I leaned forward. Miriam Baxter fascinated me. We were the same age, similar upbringing, though I was raised in upstate New York and Miriam just outside of London. But upper middle-class families, good schools, nice homes. What fork-in-the-road decision had put us both on such divergent paths? "So, you do it for the money?" I asked.

Miriam nodded. "Hell, yes. And at this point, I've got my roster of regulars. I mostly do girlfriend experiences. You know, the bloke comes round and yaps about his day while I make him feel listened to and heard. Then I stroke his ego... amongst other things."

I bit back a snort of laughter.

Miriam grinned at me and continued. "The only difference between me and some punter's actual girlfriend is I get paid for my services without any of that messy relationship nonsense."

I sat back. "Do you worry about your safety at all?"

Miriam's dark, elegantly shaped brows drew down. "I'm an escort, remember? That means I'm high class. My clients are all vetted and by referral only. Lucy, my manager, would castrate any man who laid a hand on me. It's not like I'm on the street." I smiled. "I might be a slag, but I'm a very expensive one."

"So you've never been afraid."

Miriam shook her head. "I'm sure that won't always be the case, but I refuse to live my life in fear. My decisions are my own. No one is forcing me. I look at these punters as regular guys who can't get something they need. I provide it... for a fee."

This was a world I hadn't ever given much thought to until I saw my name next to Carmen's on the cast list. "What if the client wants something really kinky?"

As I asked the question, I slid my gaze around the sleek and modern bar. We were seated off to the side, and mellow music played at a muted level. The Savoy bar was the definition of a swank London establishment, with images of pop stars immortalized in art on the walls. But while other patrons talked about their days or their relationships, we were discussing having sex for money.

"If he wants something kinky, then he calls someone else. I have a strict list of what I will and won't do that Lucy keeps track of. Occasionally a guy will want to try something, and if I'm into it I'll give it a go. But it's cleared by Lucy first, and I know to expect it in our next session. But usually, my guys are straight vanilla sex. Missionary, doggy style, girl on top. If they are feeling adventurous, we try a toy or two, but that's basically it."

"You can say no, then?"

"Yes, but I leave the nitty-gritty details to Lucy. Just because he's paying for it doesn't mean he doesn't have to answer to someone. And in this case, it's Lucy."

"She sounds formidable."

Miriam nodded. "She takes care of her girls."

I made a note to ask more about Lucy later. But first, one I was dying to know. "Are you ever attracted to any of the men?"

Miriam laughed. "Of course. I get to physically screen each of the clients myself."

Like shopping out of a magazine? "How does that work?"

"We meet in a place like this for a drink. Think of it like a job interview. He's seeing if I'm charming and smart and he likes my tits, and I'm seeing if he's balding or paunchy or I like his tips. After that initial meeting, he sets up a date."

"And if you're not into it?"

"Then I tell Lucy not in a million fucking years, and she sends someone else."

"So you look at it like dating."

Miriam grinned. "But the pay is better."

I leaned forward. "Okay, tell me. Is there anyone really hot? You know, that you'd sleep with for free."

Miriam might be my research for my role, but I liked the bawdy, brash girl and the way she was direct and open.

"Is there ever. I won't name names, but I've had famous, gorgeous pop stars and footballers. One client I have now is so beautiful to look at he makes me tongue-tied sometimes."

"If he's so beautiful, then why do you think he comes to a sex—erm, escort?"

Miriam frowned and chewed her lip. I glanced around surreptitiously to see if someone might overhear our conversation. "Honestly, I have no idea. He oozes sex appeal. And he's charming and smart. But the kicker is he doesn't ever want to sleep with me. He wants to talk. And he pays double my whole-night rate for the privilege." She shrugged. "Who knows, maybe he can't get it up."

"So you're telling me he pays an escort to 'talk' and not in a fun, euphemistic, dirty-talk kind of way?"

Miriam let out a loud bark of laughter. "Honey, I wish he *would* talk dirty to me." Several patrons in the bar turned to look. "And it's not for lack of me trying. In the two years I've been seeing him, we've never had sex."

"But you would if he wanted to?"

Miriam licked her bottom lip. "He's one client I'd sleep with free of charge."

I raised a brow. "That beautiful?"

"Yeah." She lowered her voice and leaned forward. "My limit list is strict. But I'd try just about anything he asked. He's that sexy. But all he ever wants to do is talk. And he's willing to pay two thousand quid a night for the privilege."

My mouth hung open. Was she serious right now? A couple of nights with him and I could pay in cash for my sister's Briarwood Academy tuition. *Stop it. It's not that desperate yet.* "Do you think he's able to have normal relationships?"

Miriam shrugged. "What's normal? But it's not like he's odd or anything. On the contrary, I just don't think he has anyone to talk to. I'm a little protective of him. We've become friends of a sort."

I wondered if Miriam's friend would ever take her out

and introduce her to his other friends. We talked for another two hours about everything from the worst thing she'd ever been asked to do (a client wanted to give her a golden shower) to if anyone had ever asked her to leave her job for them (twice). She hadn't taken them up on their offers.

My timer went off, and I sighed with disappointment. *Already?* How had it been two hours? "Time flies when you're having fun. Thank you so much for your time. Can I call you again if I have some more questions?" I reached into my purse for my wallet.

Miriam held out a hand. "Put your money away. I like you, so I'm not charging you. Call me anytime."

"I must admit, it's a whole fascinating other world."

"Well if you're really curious, then you should take a job yourself. You know, really embody your character."

My jaw unhinged.

My new friend laughed. "You should see your face. It's brilliant. But I'm serious."

"I couldn't."

Miriam shrugged. "Why not? It's just sex. And a pretty girl like you, you're already having it anyway, so why not get paid?"

I sputtered. "I-uh..." My voice trailed as I tried to think of something to say. "I couldn't."

Miriam waved her hand dismissively. "If you say so. But if you want to see it from the inside for your research, I have just the client. My no-dirty-talk talker. And I give my word on your personal safety. Easiest two thousand quid you ever made."

Two thousand—*No!* No. I wouldn't. But still. That was a lot of money. "Thanks, but I think I'll stick to research. I'm not a method kind of girl."

"Well, if you change your mind, you know where to find me."

CHAPTER THREE

IMANI

"Tell me the juicy bits about your meeting today. What was it like meeting a streetwalker?" My landlord, Felix, asked with a waggled eyebrow. In truth, Fe was so much more than my landlord. Over the last three years, he'd become my best friend. Hell, sometimes it felt like he was my only friend. Well, him and his boyfriend, Adam. I'd come to rely on them. Maybe too much.

His house in Kingston upon the Thames was beyond posh. He'd quartered it into four flats and completely renovated each of them into a fabulous contemporary paradise. He'd fitted the units with every modern appliance I could even conceive of, along with hardwood floors and beautiful furnishings. He lived in one and rented one to me. The other two units were rented by guys who worked in finance and I knew he charged me pennies compared to what the other two were paying.

"Escort," I laughed. "Though, she doesn't really care what I call her. She's pretty cool, actually."

"What? Are you about to have her round to supper? Don't tell me you're about to actually have another friend. I'll be jealous."

I rolled my eyes. "I'm telling you that if you met her and I didn't tell you what she did for a living, you would assume she was a student. A well-dressed student, but a student just the same. She could be me. More importantly, *I* could be *her*. It's hard not to see the similarities. Miriam said that she was a student who needed money and she liked sex, so it was a natural transition."

"Don't think I didn't notice you avoided my hint that you need some more friends."

Fe also worried over me like a mother hen. Always checking if I'd eaten or gotten enough sleep. And his latest thing was that I was too isolated, needed to branch out and go out more. Though I doubted he assumed I'd make friends with an escort.

He leaned forward on the kitchen stool, as if eager for more details. "So, does she have like a pimp and stuff? I mean, I've seen *Secret Diary*. But I assume most of that is embellished."

I gave it some thought. "You know, I'm not sure how much of it is embellished. Miriam was saying that she has a handler who screens all the clients. Clients sign up for an exclusive dating service, whether they need a date for the night for an event or a little more. Sometimes it's a date for a weekend. The client stipulates if sex will be required. Some girls don't have sex and are just companions."

"As if." He laughed. "What doddering old geezer would pay for some hot young thing and not expect to have sex?"

"I dunno. That's what I'm curious about. She walked me through the whole thing about how the dates are set up, how the girls meet the client beforehand and yea or nay them. It's really elaborate."

Fe's eyes widened with interest. "Forget Billie Piper, this is far more interesting."

"I told you, right? Miriam even suggested I give it a go."

That broke the spell. "What the fuck?" His brows drew down. "That's not fucking funny, Imani."

I held up my hands. "Hey, I'm a little impulsive, but I'm not stupid, okay? I'm not going to sleep with a stranger for money. If I'm sleeping with a stranger, I'm doing it like every other twenty-one-year-old I know. I'll meet him in a pub with beer goggles on and let him take me home."

He grinned. "That's more like it. Wait, how much did you say she made for just talking to the bloke?"

"She makes two thousand pounds a night for that guy."

"Can somebody please tell me how I can get paid like that?"

"Fe, you realize she's still an escort, right? At any time, the guy could decide he wants sex from her."

"And from what you said, he's supposedly well fit. So what's the problem? Philosophically speaking, of course. I would never let my bestie become a hooker. I'd rather pay you to be my beard than have you shag paunchy, balding men for a few bob."

I rolled my eyes. "Not that I would want to. But for that much money in one night, I can see the appeal. I mean, this girl could easily have been me. She's about my age. Pretty. Intelligent. I'm more than a little fascinated by the twists and turns that landed her where she is and me where I am."

"Don't cry for her, Argentina. She's laughing all the way to her mattress. Both literally and as her bank." He winked.

I snorted a laugh. "You're terrible. But you know what? You're right. That girl has no money problems. From her vintage Gucci dress to her Louboutins, she looked like she was made of the stuff."

"Well, apparently her vagina is," he snickered.

"You're terrib—"

He was saved by my ringing cell phone. When I jogged by him, he swatted at my bottom and I managed to just scoot out of the way. Snatching up my phone, I grinned when I saw it was my sister calling.

"Hey, Ebony. You're calling ahead of schedule. So I

can only assume—" My sister's sobbing on the other end of the call interrupted me. "Sweetie, what's the matter?"

Through her sobs, I was only able to make out words like *late notice, mortgage,* and *evicted.*

"Eb, I need you to take a deep breath and calm down. Tell me slowly." At sixteen, my sister could sometimes be melodramatic.

Over the line, I could hear Ebony's attempts to pull herself together. "I came home early and checked the mail. There was a red one from the mortgage company, so I went into Dad's office to put it on his desk where he'd see it. But there were so many letters just like it. I was worried, so I opened it. It says we're in arrears and if they don't receive payment on the back mortgage they will have no choice but to foreclose."

Blood rushed in my ears as my lungs constricted. That house was the last reminder of our mother. After her death five years ago, our father had been steadily declining, drinking more and more to keep himself functional. "Did you call Dad?"

She sniffled. "I couldn't reach him."

Fuck. I didn't need this. "Stay calm, okay? I'll take care of it."

"How? It's not like you have six grand sitting around."

Good point. But I'd think of something. This wasn't Ebony's mess to clean up. It was mine. I'd gotten a scholarship to RADA, but my father had been adamant that I stay home and attend the State University of New York for college. I'd hated leaving my sister behind, but I'd had to escape. Had to leave that dark, depressing house. Had to find some freedom and signs of life. *Look where that landed you.*

I shook off the shadow of gloom and regret. I didn't have time to wallow. I needed money, and fast. I had some saved, but that was to keep me afloat through the summer while I found an agent and hopefully a job. I wasn't tapping into that if I could help myself. *What would you do for your sister?* That answer was simple. Everything. "Look. Just tell Dad to call me, and I'll get it sorted."

"O-okay."

By the time I hung up with my sister ten minutes later, I felt desperate and drained.

Fe shook his head. "I don't like the gist of the convo I heard."

"Family drama. The usual. Just this time, my dumbass father has managed to not pay the mortgage for God knows how many months."

"Shite."

"Exactly. I hate that he leaves these messes for me and Ebony to clean up. For fuck's sake, Ebony's only sixteen."

"And how old were you when you had to pull him out of a bar by yourself?"

I wrinkled my nose. That was the problem with getting close to people, they knew all your shit. "That's beside the point. I was way more mature. I was already looking after Ebony most of the time. She deserves to hold on to what little childhood she has left."

"To be fair, she's hardly a child. Maybe she can—"

"Can what? Come up with six thousand dollars?"

Fe winced. "That's a lot of dosh."

"Tell me about it. I'm going to have to dip into my savings and get an extra job to pay for it."

"Or you could take the easy way out and let me pay."

I shifted uncomfortably. "No, Fe. We've been over this."

"Yes, we have. And I have more money than I need. And as your gay husband, I want to help."

I swiped a wayward lock out of my face. "You help already. I'm practically paying you pennies for rent. You have the best hangover cure known to mankind. And most importantly, you've been my friend. That's all I need."

I'd never met Felix's father, who apparently was some kind of lord. He was embarrassed about having an openly gay son, so he paid him to stay away. I didn't want anything to do with that money. I knew how painful it was for him to have his family reject him. He'd been in a relationship with his boyfriend, Adam, for two years, and he still didn't talk about Adam to his mother. I wanted no part of that rejection they soaked him in.

There is another way out. One where I didn't have to count on Fe's blood money.

He frowned at me. "Please tell me you're not thinking what I think you're thinking."

I shook my head and hoped I was a good enough actress to lie to my bestie. "Of course not. I'm not that crazy." No. I was that desperate.

As soon as Fe had his back turned, I texted Miriam.

Imani: *So, about that non-dirty-talking client of yours. I've changed my mind and would like to go method.*

Miriam's return text was swift.

Miriam: *I had a feeling I'd be hearing from you.*

🌿🌿

Xander

"Xander, I've been calling you since last night. Has your phone been switched off?"

Annabel. Damn, I'd meant to call her back, but I'd been too busy at uni. For the next several months, if things went according to plan, then I'd be spending less time teaching, and I needed to prep some things to transition to Abbie. "Sorry, love. Been working. What's the emergency?"

"You ask that casually like you didn't approach me about the London Artistic Trust. I swear it's like you don't even want on the board."

My gut twisted. Oh, I wanted the job. It was a vital piece in the puzzle I'd been working on for the last five years. The trust both supported the arts and sponsored several charities, in particular, charities for at-risk and endangered children who were the victims of abuse. Getting on was the only way I'd get access to files on board members, or rather one in particular.

I had my investigator, Garett Ball, looking into Alistair's past and history. I needed access to those files. I was sure I'd find complaints against Alistair from the charities I worked closely with. And the only way to get them was to get on the board. But I had a secondary reason, as well. Only a board member could call for another's dismissal. The Artistic Trust was the only charity board Alistair sat on. And I'd seen an interview once where Alistair talked about how much he loved it. And if Alistair loved something, then I wanted to strip it away. I'd been waiting for this opportunity for five long years.

And now it was within my grasp. "I want the bloody job."

"Then you need to start making yourself bleeding available."

"I'm sorry, Annabel. I'm all yours."

"What? Xander Chase is capable of apology?"

"I'm capable. I'm just not often wrong."

"Next time, make sure your bloody phone is on. You said this was important to you."

We might have been the same age, but sometimes she acted like my mother. If she were any other woman, I'd cut her loose. But in this case, she was right. I needed her.

Needed onto this board. And she'd pulled every string she could think of to get me this far. A position on the board was typically passed down in families. It was rare that the President, Jean LeClerc, allowed outsiders in. With my family connections, I could have pulled my own strings, but I didn't want my family anywhere near this. The controversy ignited would ruin everything. "Okay, fair enough, so what do you need?"

"It's more like what do *you* need. I got a personal call from LeClerc yesterday. He thinks you're an excellent fit. And they'd like to slot you into a creative director-type of capacity."

Adrenaline pumped through my veins. This was it. The next domino stacking into place. After five years I was finally getting what I wanted. The seeds of challenge started planting themselves, taking hold.

I kept my voice even. I didn't want Annabel digging too deep into why I'd wanted this job. "When do I meet with them?"

"There's a problem, Xander."

My throat constricted. I had the pedigree. But had my past come back to haunt me? There might have been rumors of what happened in my childhood home. Of how Silas McMahon had died. Of what Lex and I had done. But my father had long buried the truth. "What is it?" I asked, my voice hoarse.

She sighed. "Alistair McMahon."

Oh, he wasn't a problem. Or rather he wouldn't be once I'd dealt with him. No point in destroying a man when he couldn't stand and watch. "What about him?"

"Well, he *is* a problem. Or at the very least has convinced LeClerc that *you* are a problem. That your past history with women is not what the trust wants associated with its image."

I smirked. It's not like I hadn't expected Alistair to put up a fight. "I'll meet with LeClerc. Once he sits down with me, it'll be hard to argue that I'm not the best fit."

"You're going to need more than your charm, Xander. I'm afraid they are seriously concerned. I don't know what you did to McMahon, but he's dead set against you and is trying everything he can to make sure they don't bring you on. Lucky for you, you're good at what you do. LeClerc intimated that if there was some way to be sure you'd settled down, your past wouldn't be a question. He wants you to join them at their annual retreat in a couple of weeks in Paris."

Settled down? *Bollocks.* "Look, it won't be a problem. Tell them I have a girlfriend."

Annabel coughed. "Is that true?"

I almost choked. "Fuck no, but it'll get my foot in the door, right?"

"Xander, LeClerc may be a geezer, but he's not an idiot. He'll see through a ploy like that. Besides, you'll eventually need to produce one. Preferably, take one to

Paris with you. Significant others are allowed and encouraged."

I was hardly prepared to materialize the perfect girl-friend out of thin air. Especially one who didn't expect complicated entanglements. "Sod it. I'll sort it out."

She sighed. "I know you won't listen to me, but maybe this time you should. Go out, find a nice girl. Someone wholesome looking who will play along and who will *hang around*. At least for a bit. You'll have to produce her from time to time for it to not seem like a ploy. You don't want to get booted just as soon as you get on."

She had a point there. While LeClerc might appreciate my gumption, he wouldn't like being made a fool of. "Would you relax and let me worry about that? Believe it or not, I occasionally know what I'm doing." It looked like I would be paying Miriam a visit. I belatedly wondered how she would do with *wholesome*.

CHAPTER FOUR

IMANI

There was no way I could do this. I paced the long foyer of the posh Notting Hill flat. Yeah, sure I needed the money. *And* it was good research, but this was stupid. I knew it was stupid. But here I was, wearing a dress that probably cost more than this term's tuition with shoes that made my mouth water and my pocketbook ache. I didn't really have anything appropriate, so Miriam had lent me some clothes.

There is no sex. There is no sex. I checked the large clock on the far wall. If I was going to run, I'd better do it in the next ten minutes. I dragged in a deep breath. *Relax. Miriam said he never wants to have sex. He only wants to talk.*

I tried to picture myself as an extremely well-paid therapist, just chatting away with a client. What therapists did

I know that wore La Perla and Jimmy Choo? While the tiny voice tried to speak up, tried to convince me of my madness, the daredevil inside me tried to be calm. *He's just going to talk. All you have to do is be yourself and find out about him. Sex is not on the menu.*

Besides, I had pepper spray. Actually, make that several cans of pepper spray. I'd left them around the flat in case I got into a situation I couldn't get out of. Strictly speaking, they weren't legal in the UK, but desperate times and all that.

I tried to remember everything Miriam had told me. "Be yourself. Be calm. Let him talk about himself. Don't talk about yourself. He'll be surprised and perhaps not that thrilled to see a replacement, but if you get him talking, he'll relax."

You can do this. You're brave. This is for Ebony.

The clock chimed nine. The soft dongs of the bells made my stomach pitch. Now or never. I couldn't have run even if I wanted to. When I heard the scratching at the lock of the front door, I was powerless to move, completely frozen at my spot near the window seat. Before leaving, Miriam had dimmed the lights of the flat and lit candles to make the hypermodern flat seem more relaxed. It looked awfully romantic to me.

"Miriam?" A deep, raspy voice called from the front door. The smooth quality of it washed over my flesh, warming me from the inside. "Are you here?"

That voice. It made my skin tingle. Smoothing a hand down my dress, I sucked in a breath, then released it slowly. As the heavy footfalls approached, I tried to swallow, but I couldn't get around the sawdust. I shifted to the left in my staggering heels and tried to peer around the pillar. I stumbled slightly, and my dress caught on a hook on the wall. *Damn it.* The dress probably cost more than my rent. I didn't need to come up with the mortgage *and* have to pay Miriam back for ruining her fancy dress. I wiggled and a stitch ripped. *Oh shit.* I immediately stopped moving. I was going to tear the dress off my body if I moved.

The lights flickered on to full power, and I held my breath as I lifted my gaze to meet the most astonishing set of slate-gray eyes I'd ever seen—deep set and surrounded by thick, sooty lashes. Sandy blond hair, an angular jaw, high cheekbones and pouty mouth completed the picture of that amazing face. And the body, tall, lean and rangy. He was beautiful. There was no way this guy was the talker. He oozed sex appeal in spades. "Oh God."

He spoke at the same time through clenched teeth. "Who the fuck are you, and where the fuck is Miriam?"

Shit. "You probably hear this all the time, but this is not what it looks like."

Tall and beautiful cocked his head, and his lips twitched into the hint of a smile. "You mean you're not a beautiful girl in my flat, uninvited, wearing a handkerchief of a dress then?"

I shook my head. "Nope. All a figment of your imagination. But while you're imagining things, could you, uh, maybe help me unhook myself? I'm sort of stuck, and I don't want to rip this dress. It costs more than my flat."

He raised a brow. "So if you move, that dress rips right off of you?"

I sputtered. "What? No. Look, if you help me get loose, I'll get out of your hair and you and Miriam can reschedule."

His intense gaze roved over my body. "Okay. On one condition."

I swallowed hard. Was he going to ask for something kinky? Besides just wanting to talk? "What's that?"

"You tell me who you are."

☙ ❧

Xander

My body locked into position as lust, closely followed by confusion and anger, flooded my veins. My brain fired off a stream of questions as I tried to make sense of the situation. Instead of Miriam, this girl with the wide, hazel eyes stood in my Notting Hill flat.

Who the fuck was she? And why did she make my muscles bunch and my skin tight and itchy? From where I stood, the faint hint of coconut and hibiscus tickled my nostrils. The way the moonlight hit her honey-brown skin, she looked luminescent. And God knew that dress didn't cover enough. Or maybe it covered too much. Admittedly that last thought was just... wrong on so many levels. And why the fuck did I care what her name was?

I didn't need that kind of shit at the moment. What I needed was Miriam. I had just over a week to find someone suitable to take to Paris. I could kill her for pulling this shit. We had an arrangement. It didn't include substitutions. "Are you going to make me repeat myself? Or are you going to tell me your name?" Her eyes went wide at my raised voice, forcing me to modulate my tone and bite back a curse. "Please."

She blinked several times, causing her long lashes to just dust her cheekbones. "Uh, Jasmine. Like I said, there was a mix-up, and if you can just help me then I'll be out of your way. No harm, no foul."

"You're American?" I asked with a cocked head.

"What? The accent gave me away?"

There it was again. That twitchy thing my lips kept doing. Why did she make me want to laugh when all I really wanted to do was strangle Miriam? "For all I know you could be from Canada."

"Eh?" She nodded and muttered with a rueful smile.

This time, there was no stopping the chuckle that escaped. As I shook my head, I wondered just how crazy this girl was. For starters, she didn't look like a Jasmine and secondly, she was *no* escort. There was something real about her. She wasn't manufactured. She wasn't hard and world-weary or too sophisticated. She could make me laugh. "So tell me, Jasmine from Canada, what's a nice Canadian girl like you doing working as an escort?"

"What are the chances you'll believe I'm working my way through school?"

"About as much as me believing your name is Jasmine."

She licked her bottom lip, drawing all my focus to its fullness. "Look. This was a mistake. Just forget I was here."

Considering she was the reason I was here, that was unlikely to happen. "You realize a nice girl like you could get hurt playing around like this?" I spread my hands. "Was this Miriam's idea?"

Her brows furrowed, even as her chin tilted stubbornly. "Look, Miriam said it was supposed to be a no-stress kind of thing. I'm sorry. I really am." She covered her face with her hands. "Just help me get unhooked and I'll go. You clearly don't want me here anymore than I want to be here, so..." Her voice trailed off.

"Who said I don't want you here?" I stood rooted to the gleaming hardwood floor as the truth seeped inside my skull. I did want her there. It was the first time I'd laughed properly in weeks. Not to mention, there was something about her that made her accessible. Easy to connect to.

She was completely guileless and wanted nothing from me. Too bad that made me want *her*. Her sassy attitude, her wide eyes and a mouth that looked like it was hand-made to suck my cock had me itching to touch her. *Stop it. What the fuck is wrong with you?* I hadn't planned on having sex. Though, someone should probably tell my cock that, because the fucker was starting to swell in my jeans.

There was no way Miriam would do this to me. I'd made it clear I needed to see her. Why the fuck would she do this when I needed her? *You've never tried to sleep with her before.* I spun on my heel. This was so fucked up on so many levels.

Some of the tension rolled off her shoulders. "D-do you need to talk? Miriam said you would want to."

That broke the spell. Soon, Jasmine, or whatever her name was, would have questions about why I was seeing an escort to talk, and I didn't need that headache. "No, I don't need to talk. I'll release you, and then we can promptly forget we met, yeah?"

"Fine by me."

"Just one thing, though, I want your word that you're not going to do this again. You're not cut out to be an escort." I strode toward her, tossing the envelope of Miriam's usual payment on the mantel. I stopped when I was just a foot away from her. The coconut-and-hibiscus scent was even more potent up close. Was it her shampoo?

Damn, it made me want to nuzzle her hair. It was official. I had issues.

"Trust me, I won't. I've had enough of walking on the wild side."

I reached for her but stopped before I touched her shoulder, my blood going thick and my voice dropping an octave. "Is that why you're here? To walk on the wild side?"

Her head reared back. "No. I thought I could do this. But I can't." Wiggling a little, she raised her brows pointedly. "A little help, please."

I muttered a curse and tried to reach behind her without touching her, but no dice. My motions just made another stitch rip. "Why the second thoughts? I'm not your type?"

A strangled laugh escaped her pretty, pink lips. "Really? Someone as good-looking as you is fishing for compliments now? Why don't you tell me why you're even here to see an escort if all you want to do is talk? I'm at a loss for why. But hey, it's your prerogative. No judgment."

I cocked my head. "Somehow, that expression on your face looks an awful lot like judgment. I've seen that look on my mother's face enough to recognize it." Standing so close, I could see the flecks of green in her hazel eyes. And even better, I could tell that even though she was slim, those curves of hers weren't enhanced but were enough to overflow my big hands. The evil side of my brain conjured an image of me fucking those honey-brown tits. What color would her nipples be? *Mocha?* An even more alluring image replaced it. This one had me fucking her ass cheeks. My cock sliding between the firm, oil-slick globes as I held on tight to her flesh. *Fuck!* I was a dirty boy. And fuck if I didn't want to show her just how dirty.

I shook my head to rid myself of the image. *Release her and fucking find Miriam.*

She nodded, and her hair brushed my cheek. "Is that why you're seeing escorts? Mommy issues?"

My muscles went tight as I fought to keep from nuzzling and inhaling deep. God, she smelled good. "You have a smart mouth for a Yank."

She glowered at me. "And you have pretty teeth for a Brit."

She licked her lips again, and the action made my mouth water. I wanted to kiss the sass right off of her. Swaying a little, I said, "I needed Miriam."

"Sorry, you got me instead. And since you don't want to talk—"

I studied her intently as both hands reached behind her. With my body pressed flush against hers, my fingers worked the material over the hook. "Who said I wanted to *talk* to Miriam?"

Jasmine immediately attempted to flatten herself into the wall, but unfortunately for both of us, all she managed to do was trap my hands and bring our bodies closer together. I frowned and halted momentarily. "I'm not—" I shook my head. "I wouldn't hurt you."

"Isn't that what the praying mantis says just before biting off the head of its mate?" Despite her question, she relaxed again.

The corner of my lips tipped up in a sardonic smile as I resumed my extrication. "Consider it foreplay."

She stiffened again. "On second thought, I'll just get myself free."

"You're stuck. I'm just trying to release you so you can get out of my flat." I softened my voice. "Maybe, since I'm pretty sure you can clock my heart rate, you tell me your real name?"

"I—" She sighed. "It's Imani."

"See, how bad was that? I'm Alexander." She licked her lips, and my gaze narrowed on her mouth. "Fuck, you're really going to have to stop doing that."

She shifted on her feet. "I'm nervous. It's not like I'm doing it on purpose."

I shook my head and peered around her at the hook. There was no way to get her off the damn thing without pressing into her. "Doesn't matter," I muttered.

I sucked in a deep breath and with it the scent of her. I could feel my pulse beating a tattoo under my skin. The closer I stood to her, the choppier my breathing became. *Want.* I needed to unhook her and get the hell away from her. My cock, however, disagreed. Vehemently. *Need.* I reached around her and tried to gently pry the fabric off the hook, and hearing a stitch tear, I stopped. The only way to get her off was to lift her. *Her body pressed flush up against mine.* On no planet was that a good idea.

I clenched my jaw hard as I wrapped my arms around her and lifted her smoothly off her feet. Her body molded against me like a spray-on tan. *Want. Need.* I managed to unhook her and set her feet back on the ground, but not before sliding her all the way down my body. Every curve of hers pressed against me and I wanted to do a lot more to her tits than just fuck them. Like lick, suckle, and tease until her eyes rolled back into her head with pleasure. I needed to step away from her. The last thing I needed was a complication. But every command my brain gave went unheeded.

"You're a little close, aren't you?" Her voice was soft.

Another chuckle escaped my lips. "I'm not sure you understand how this is supposed to go."

She swallowed hard. "Oh, I understand the mechanics, but..." She paused, not sure how to put it. "You said that you didn't want to... uh... talk."

I reached out and smoothed a lock of her hair between my fingers. "I think I changed my mind. I *do* want to talk. But there's something about you that makes me want to touch too."

"You should realize that touching a woman's hair is a really personal thing."

"So is standing in a man's flat wearing a dress made for sin, fuck-me heels, and a smile."

"To be fair, I wasn't smiling." She rocked from foot to foot. "You're still standing too close."

I laughed low. "And you still don't seem to know how this works."

My skin tingled just from her proximity, and need pulled low in my belly. "Imani?"

Gaze heavy-lidded, she mumbled, "Hmmm?"

"I'm going to kiss you now."

CHAPTER FIVE

XANDER

My hands shook as the blood rushed in my ears. *What. The. Hell. Are. You. Doing?* The voice in my skull called louder and louder until I couldn't concentrate.

A wave of lust washed through me. The force of it strong enough to make my hands shake. Fuck, I wanted her. So damn bad. What was so special about *this* girl?

Oh, I'd wanted women before. *Lots* of women. But this was different. It wasn't just her body. She made me laugh. Her sharp tongue turned me on almost as much as her insane body did. If this girl so much as breathed on me, I could lose control. And instead of running, I was threatening to kiss the source of danger?

With her lips slightly parted, Imani blinked wide eyes up at me. I couldn't be sure, but she looked like she was holding her breath. Was she scared? Was she just as confused as I was?

When I inched closer, she let out a little puff of air, and I couldn't hold back the groan. Sliding my hands into her hair and fisting the strands at the nape of her neck, I dragged her to me and slid my lips over hers.

God, she tasted sweet... with just a hint of bite. She was perfect. Cupping the back of her neck allowed my tongue to slide into her warm depths and explore. Blood rushed in my ears, driving me to take more. So much more. I needed to get closer, needed to feel her respond.

The change in her was like ice slowly melting. When she finally kissed me back, sliding her tongue over mine, I moaned. Desire rode the back of debilitating need as I licked into her mouth, desperate to consume her.

When she gasped, I took full advantage, pressing closer against her, relishing in every lush curve against my body. Tiny pinpricks of pain alerted me that she was grabbing onto my biceps, but I didn't care. It didn't matter how much I took, the hunger didn't sate. My body vibrated, and the base of my spine tingled with a pleasant hum. All the while my cock begged to be released, to be stroked, to be touched.

Finally, Imani made a little mewling sound at the back of her throat, and she slid her arms around my neck. *Fuck, yes.* I drew her closer, my erection pressing against her belly. When her tongue slid over mine, tentatively tasting, I growled low in my throat and my hand fisted tighter.

Somewhere in the back of my mind, I registered the tightening of my balls. What the fuck? I wanted to come? She was so soft and tasted like velvety ice-cream on a hot summer day, going down smooth and refreshing, making me want more.

I dragged my lips from hers, but her fingers wound into the hair at the nape of my neck, tugging me closer. The only brain cells I had left were the two rubbing together, but I had to ask. If she said yes, I'd let her go, even if it killed me. "Do you want me to stop?"

Imani's tongue moistened her lower lip and she dragged heavy lids open to meet my gaze. She waited several moments before answering, then, slowly, she shook her head from side to side.

"Thank fuck." I dipped my head again and nibbled at her lips until she parted them on a sigh and her tongue slid over mine easily. Her body molded even more tightly to me as she stood on tiptoes in an effort to bring us closer.

Control. I needed to find some goddamned control. All I had to do was relax a little. *Don't rush.* But fuck, I wanted to rush. She was rubbing her body against me, writhing in my arms, and I wanted to do lots of other things to elicit that reaction.

Imani arched her back, and the last tenuous hold I had on my control evaporated.

Picking her up easily, I blindly marched into the bedroom and deposited her in the middle of the bed without breaking the kiss. Well aware of how much smaller she was, I was careful not to lay my whole weight over her. Instead, I shifted us to our sides and settled her against me fully. With a rough groan, I hiked up a handful of her dress, exposing her flesh to my hands.

"Fuuuuck." She felt so good. The command my brain gave to slow down was at direct war with my body's *Yes, right there,* murmurs. The tingling in my spine spread quickly, and the thundering roar of my heartbeat drowned out any other sound but her moans, mewls and little gasps.

Frustration riding me, I shifted our bodies again so I could yank my shirt over my head before settling myself back against her. My cock aligned against the hot center of her body and I bit back a moan when Imani lifted her hips into mine.

I dropped my forehead to hers, breaking the kiss. I gnashed my teeth together while I tried to quiet the tornado of emotions. With a feather-soft touch, she cupped my cheek and kissed me softly. There was something so tender, unguarded, and vulnerable about her in that moment, and I was lost. Her soft touch was enough to force honesty out of me. "What are you doing to me? I am so desperate to be inside of you right now." I wanted this. For more than just one night. This was what it was supposed to feel like. I knew, because I'd been missing it in warm but emotionally empty beds for years.

Her fingers drifted down my face, over my collarbone. From the ring I wore on a chain around my neck to my pecs. I whispered, "Fuck," as she grazed my nipple. It made her smile. Sliding lower, she traced each of my abs as if counting them. But it wasn't until she traced her fingers over my happy trail that I started to shake. Shit, I had to get myself under control. But it was like we were in a cocoon of fog where only this moment in time mattered.

I released her and in record time shed my belt, leaving my pants hanging low on my hips. When was the last time I'd felt like this? Actually wanted someone just because it felt good? I didn't want to rush this. I didn't want to lose the way it felt. Didn't want it to evaporate.

When I slid back into bed, I gripped her hips reflexively as I kissed her again, rolling my hips into hers. The only sounds permeating the room were our gasps and groans as I devoured her with my mouth. From the way my skin hummed everywhere she touched me, I knew sliding into her would be heaven. I knew we would be combustible. Knew that she would own me. Because a small part of her did already.

Imani arched into my body with a satisfied groan when I captured her breast in my palm, filling my hand and then some. I teased the peak with my thumb, moaning in satisfaction when it pebbled under my thumb. I wanted her crazy for me, desperate for release, desperate for connection. I wanted her to feel what I felt.

"Fuck, this has to go." With an impatient yank, I dragged her dress up. Imani fumbled with the straps and I stilled her hands. "Let me." Her hands shook as they fell away and her gaze never left mine. Deftly, I unsnapped the hooks holding the dress together on her slim shoulders and tugged it up over her head.

She lay back, and my eyes devoured every inch of her from her firm, toned legs to the lush curve of her hips, to her flat stomach with the hint of a six-pack. But my focus strayed to her full breasts and dark nipples peeking at me behind delicate lace. I dipped my head, teasing the nipple by blowing a warm breath across the peak, and her breath caught.

When I grazed the tip with my teeth, Imani laced her fingers into my hair and tugged me closer, as if willing me to take her into my mouth, to suckle her. It wasn't until I wrapped my lips around the nipple that she rocked her heated core along my cock, stroking me with the satin and lace of her panties. Teasing me with the promised heat and slickness of her pussy.

My hands coasted up her silky-smooth thigh to the elastic of the flimsy material. Shifting the fabric aside, I stroked my fingers over her slippery folds. As soon as my questing fingers tentatively dipped inside her, she raked her fingers over my scalp and a harsh cry tore from her throat.

I retracted my finger then stroked her again, sliding my finger further. With each glide, I took more of her. Eventually adding another finger as my palm rubbed over her clit. I wanted her as mine. Wanted to know that *I'd* made her come. "That's it, Angel, come for me, don't hold back. I want to see it. I need your pussy milking my fingers—your slickness coating them. Show me what you'll do to my cock when I fuck you."

She dragged her eyes open and blinked up at me, our gazes locking as her back bowed. She was coming—and she was fucking incredible. As if timed perfectly to hers, my body fought against the restraint I tried to apply.

Fuck. Oh God. Blinding light danced on the edges of my vision. As quivers wracked her body and her pussy pulsed around my fingers like they were my cock, I felt pleasure with the force of a tsunami chasing up my spine. *No. No, no, no.*

Not now, not like this. I wanted to be *inside* her.

Fuck it. I'd never had a moment like this in my life, I wasn't going to try to stop it. Not that I could.

Even though I tried to will it from happening, I came— hard. And all I could do was hold her against me tightly for support as my whole body shook. The only sound that registered with me was the sound of my name on Imani's tongue.

CHAPTER SIX

IMANI

Pulsing, throbbing heat between my thighs woke me out of a dead-sleep stupor. My body hummed with electricity. My skin felt alive, and between my thighs, I throbbed, needing... something.

Oh fuck. My eyelids snapped open, but I lay perfectly still. What the hell had I done? *Dry-humped Mr. No-Dirty-Talk. Oh God.* And what was worse, dry humping him and letting him get me off was far hotter than anything I'd ever experienced in my life. By miles. No, actually, what was worse was he thought I was an escort. *Fantastic.*

I had to get out of there, had to get home. My mind raced as images of the night before came back to me, one by one. What I wore, how I acted, the way Xander had looked at me. The way he'd sucked on my nipples, touched me, and demanded that I come.

I tried to sit up, but a steel vise held me in place against a heated brick wall.

No, not a wall. Xander's chest. *Holy fuck*, his body was *unreal*. Last night I'd been so distracted by the sensations in my body, I hadn't taken the time to properly admire his.

"Morning," he whispered.

I froze. For the first time in my life, I had no idea what to say. I had absolutely no words for the situation. I cleared my throat. If I stayed calm, I could get up and go. "Uh, hi."

"You're about to run from me, aren't you?" His chest rumbled against my back.

Hell yes. "No. Uh, of course not. I just wanted a drink. I'm thirsty."

His chuckle was low and raspy. "You're a terrible liar. I know an escape when I see one."

I tried to wiggle free, but he held me still. "Can you let me go, please?"

His lips grazed my nape before he spoke. "Relax, I'm going to let you up. Just... give me a minute."

He held me tighter, and I resisted the urge to melt into him. This was the harsh light of day, not the cover of night in romantic lighting. Last night I'd been caught up in him. The way he smelled, the way he moved. How he touched me. And all that tension I'd been carrying around dissipated. It had felt great to forget—for a night. To pretend I wasn't myself. And if I was honest, he made me want things. Things I hadn't thought about since I'd had my heart and my trust shattered.

I knew I'd never get out of his grip until he was ready to let me go. When I relaxed marginally, he asked, "What perfume are you wearing? It's been driving me mad. I'm not entirely sure if it's your shampoo or your perfume."

"It's called 'Don't get me wrong, baby, but I don't swallow.'"

There was a beat of silence, then another, and his cock twitched against my ass. When he spoke, his voice was so low I barely heard the words. "Tell me, Angel, do you swallow?"

"What's the point of going down on someone if you don't swallow?" A hot flush crept over my skin. Oh God, I needed a muzzle. I needed to watch my dirty mind around him. Actually, no, I didn't, because the second I was out of here, I was never going to see him again. I was not going to have this conversation. Not half naked and locked in his embrace. "I thought you were going to let me go?"

He loosened his grip on me slightly. "I am. I, uh... need to clean up. I would have done it..." His voice trailed off and he cleared his throat. "I would have, you know, after, but I was afraid you'd vanish on me if I took a shower. And I thought maybe we should... talk."

He was certainly astute, because that *had* been my plan, if I hadn't passed the hell out. Last night was the most I'd relaxed in God only knew how long. "Oh." I rolled into his arms to face him, and I was struck by the sheer beauty of his features. I'd had one long-term boyfriend in my life and a couple of drunken pub hookups, but none of them had the same gravitational pull on me that he did. He looked like he was carved by the masters, and those silvery eyes were both arresting and haunting. Not to mention, he certainly knew his way around a woman's body. This guy didn't have erectile dysfunction, and he clearly wasn't gay. There was no way a guy like him *needed* an escort. So what was he doing setting appointments with Miriam? *Not your biz.*

His gaze lingered on my mouth, and I sucked in my bottom lip. That was the intensity that had landed me in his bed in the first place. *Stay.* No. *Fuck* no. I would not be staying. To become some clichéd song? I didn't have to see him ever again. I could just forget that I'd temporarily lost my damn mind.

"I don't... we don't... need to talk. I'm not that girl. I'm not going to show up here demanding that you spend time with me or whatever."

Xander sighed and dropped his forehead to mine. "I'm going to get a quick shower, and then I'd like to talk to you. I have something I want to ask you. Please promise you're not going to disappear on me yet. It's important."

There was a vulnerability about him that tugged at me. He was certainly all man, as evidenced by the erection nudging my belly, the hard planes of his chest, and his mouthwatering abs. But in the early-morning light, there was childlike openness about him. It pulled at my nurturing instincts. Unable to speak, I nodded.

He released a long breath and finally let me go. "I'll only be a minute, okay?"

"Yeah, okay."

He stood smoothly, and it was clear he took care of his body. And Jesus, fuck me, Christ, that ass was a thing of perfection, with those pinstriped pants hanging loosely off his hips. He didn't turn before entering the adjoining bathroom.

When the door to the bathroom clicked shut, I sighed. He wanted me to stay. Wanted to talk to me. But the threads of niggling doubt infiltrated my mind. What was there to talk about really?

It didn't matter; I couldn't stay. This was not a guy I could date. For starters, he frequented prostitutes. Secondly, I got the impression that though he wanted me, he wasn't particularly pleased about it. And finally, the last thing I needed was another Ryan situation. The moment the thought about my ex floated to the surface, I ruthlessly suppressed it again. This guy was not Ryan. He didn't scare me, but there was an edge to him that should. Maybe if I'd paid closer attention to that edge in Ryan, I wouldn't have ended up where I did.

He is not Ryan. Logically I knew that. Maybe he wouldn't hurt me like Ryan had, but I certainly wasn't taking that risk again. Last night had been a fluke. A stupid moment I wouldn't be repeating.

I shivered as my brain started fully functioning. There was the little matter of me taking Miriam's place last night. Essentially, I'd been there to render services for money. I'd slept with him. Okay, maybe not technically, but I'd gotten him off for money. As far as he was concerned, I was an escort.

I swallowed hard. The conflicting emotions of shame and desire warred for attention. I'd needed that money, still needed it, but this wasn't me. Sliding my glance at the envelope on the mantel with the colorful pound notes spilling out, I shuddered. What we'd done last night hadn't been about money. I couldn't take it.

I sat up quickly, and my abdominal muscles protested. So did my hip flexors. It had been a long time since I'd used them in any fashion pertaining to sex. I threw the covers off, shivering in the early-morning air. But now wasn't the time to focus on my chilly toes, it was the time to get the hell up and out of dodge before I had to face my decisions in the cold light of day.

After dressing quickly, I left the envelope where it lay on the mantel and strode out of the flat as quickly as I could before I was tempted to take it. There had to be another way, and I'd find it.

Xander

Something was wrong. I knew it the moment I got out of the shower. She was gone. But knowing it didn't stop me from calling out for her. "Imani? Are you here?" My heart tripped as I stalked into the bedroom with the towel slung low on my hips.

The bed was still rumpled, and my dick twitched just thinking about how we'd messed it up. But no Imani. To be sure, I ran into the sitting room to see if she was still there, but no luck. "Fuck."

On the mantel, the envelope full of cash sat where I'd laid it. Picking it up, I slapped it against my thigh before sinking down on the couch. I'd held her for hours during the night, afraid she'd vanish into the ether. Afraid that I'd wake up to find her gone, having only imagined the night before. I'd even convinced myself that maybe she would go to Paris with me. I'd thought I could hire her. But I looked at the money clutched in my fist, and it became even clearer to me that she was no escort.

That was the first orgasm I'd had with another person in years, and she'd walked out on me as if she didn't feel anything last night. *It doesn't matter.* So what if she'd run? Not like there weren't plenty of women in London. If I'd come with her, I could come with someone else. Maybe it was all over. Maybe I was cured now. *Wishful thinking.*

"Fuck. Fuck. Fuck." But she was the one I wanted. *Too bloody bad. You can't have her.* I'd be better off if I could forget her. Maybe last night had nothing to do with her. *Liar.* Though there was one way to find out.

This was so fucked up. Why her? And why now? When I was so close to getting everything I wanted. She was a hell of a complication I didn't need. I had a plan, and chasing after this girl wasn't part of it.

Remember what happened the last time you chased after a girl? Yeah. I'd been gutted because Christie hadn't had any faith in me.

When I was younger, I'd wondered how fucked up all the shit in my past had made me. Early psychologists had told me that just because I'd been abused by my mother's boyfriend didn't make me gay, nor did it mean there was anything shameful about sex.

Logically I knew that. Had known it. I liked girls. *Lots* of girls. And life had been just fine. I'd buried the past and set a mental dragon to guard the dungeon in case it ever tried to escape. I might have taken a little advantage, especially when I was younger, sleeping with every model I could get my hands on. Every city I'd been to, I'd never slept alone unless I chose to. It might have felt a little empty, but I could function and survive. Eventually I'd fallen for someone and started to settle down.

But everything had changed five years ago after I saw Silas's son again. Alistair had apparently been living in the states for some time and had just returned to London. Once we met, the past refused to stay buried. The nightmares had started. And the women... I'd never forget that night.

Alistair had approached me at a benefit party acting like we were long-lost pals. He'd had the gall to pretend he hadn't helped destroy my life and Lex's life. As if he hadn't deliberately shattered me from the inside. Alistair had vowed to ruin me if I kept spouting lies about him. And he'd given me a taste of how bad it could be.

A week after the benefit, I went home to find Alistair coming out of my place. That twat had told my fiancée just enough about my past for her to doubt me. She didn't have enough faith in me to believe me, to stand by me. With Christie gone, I spiraled out of control. It hasn't been pretty. There were so many women, too many, as I tried to fill the void Christie left. But after several months of trying to fuck myself into a stupor, the women became faceless, nameless, warm bodies. And then one night I couldn't come at all.

Good thing it didn't take me long to realize that I could come on my own just fine, but not with company. So I'd found a way to cope. Even if I *had* wanted a relationship, there was no way I'd want anyone close to that secret. Or the shame I felt after every time I made myself come.

There was no shame last night. Goddamn it. I had to stop. I'd felt more alive in one night than I had in a long time. Screw what she could do to my body with just a look. I wasn't going there again.

I checked the clock and swore. I was late for the RADA shoot with Abbie. I needed to get my shit together. I was supposed to be training her.

I dressed quickly then snagged my phone out of my coat pocket. Six missed calls. Two of them from Abbie. *Bollocks.* With the phone braced in position between my shoulder and my ear, I shoved my feet into my shoes.

Concern laced Abbie's voice when she answered. "Xander, are you okay?"

She was worried about me? An uneasy feeling rolled through me. What the hell was that? Guilt? It was foreign; I didn't recognize it at first. I shoved it aside. "Yeah, all right."

She breathed a long sigh then said, "I've been worried about you. It's not like you to be late. We're supposed to be at RADA for the shoot in an hour."

"Sorry, love." I almost bit back the word, but fuck it. "I overslept. I'll be there in twenty."

"Okay, I'll wait."

Guilt—so not an emotion I wanted to repeat. Not a fan at all. I made it a point to be on time to things for her. She was there to learn from me, and I didn't like robbing her of that time.

Also, you're half in love with her. Your brother's fiancée. Except the usual sickening feeling that lurked in the pit of my stomach when I thought of Abbie had eased somewhat. My mind conjured up an image of Imani, and I groaned.

"Xander, you sure you're okay? We don't have to do this today. I'll call and reschedule."

"No, I'm sure. I'm on my way. Wait for me, please."

There was a beat of silence. "Uh, okay. But, you're okay though?"

I knew why she was asking. In less than thirty seconds, I'd already said both *please* and *sorry*. It was unlike me. "Yep, just knackered. On my way." I hung up with her before I could say anything stupid.

As I ran out the door, I rang Miriam. She answered on the first ring. "Xander, what the fuck?"

"You're taking the piss, right? You sent me a replacement last night."

"Yeah, well, you weren't supposed to shag her. She wasn't a bloody escort. Just a friend who needed the dosh."

"Miriam, this is so fucked up." I pinched the bridge of my nose as I unlocked my car. "Is she—" I swallowed hard as the question filtered through my brain. "Is she okay? She sort of skipped out on me."

"I didn't talk to her. She just left me a message that said she wouldn't be doing that again and that she'd left the money behind." She gave a mirthless chuckle. "In the two years you've been coming to me, you've never shagged me. God, I swore you were gay. It was the only reason I sent her."

Gay? Seriously? "No. Not gay. And I didn't shag her." I slid into the front seat of my Pagani Huayra. "Not exactly,

---

---

anyway. Look. It's complicated. Do you know how I can find her?" Fuck, I sounded like a desperate twat. *That's because you are a desperate twat.*

"I have her number, but there's no way I'm giving it to you without her permission."

Fuck. "Get her fucking permission and give it to me. I need to talk to her." I needed to do a lot more than talk to her. My gut twisted. What the hell was so special about her? She was beautiful, sure, but it was more than that.

"Fine, I'll ask. What was so urgent you wanted to see me last night anyway?"

Paris. But did I still want to take her? Last night, while I'd been holding Imani, my sex-dazed brain had entertained the possibility that *she* could go with me. If that was even her name. At least I wouldn't have to fake a connection to someone while under that kind of scrutiny. *At least I wouldn't have to be alone.*

"I'll talk to you about it later." *You need her.* Maybe not. I might find Imani first.

CHAPTER SEVEN

IMANI

"**Y**ou don't have to be nervous, you know. It's going to be great. You're my star."

I rolled my shoulders and forced a smile for my director and mentor, Charles Adams. Without him, I probably never would have made it through the program. "I'm hardly a star, Charles. I'll be less nervous if you just tell me who my costar is." It had been announced nearly two weeks ago that I would be starring as Carmen. But at the time of my announcement, they had still been looking for the male lead. It wasn't uncommon to use an alumnus. My vote was for Matthew Macfadyen or Tom Hiddleston if that were the case. Though I was not possibly that lucky.

"Nonsense. You have to start believing it, my girl."

I shrugged. "I'm not looking to be a star. I just want to

breathe life into my characters to the best of my ability and get paid for what I love."

"And that will be good enough," he said with a paternal grin. The man was more of a father to me than my own. "You don't have to wait any longer." With my arm looped into his, I let him lead me down the auditorium stairs of the rehearsal hall to the stage.

"I can't believe you've been keeping the male lead such a secret."

He chuckled. "I wasn't allowed to say anything because I didn't know if we could get him released from his current filming obligations in time, but here he is. I believe you are already familiar with Ryan Ellison."

My step faltered at the sound of the name, making Charles take the final step without me. As a result, I stumbled into the one person I never wanted to see again. Ryan was technically a student at RADA, but he'd put his studies on hold for a BBC series. After the series, he'd gotten a big Spielberg film. He was a huge star now. He was also my ex, the one person with the power to hurt and destroy me.

I reflexively flinched from his touch when he reached out to steady me. *Run. Say something. Anything.* This was not happening. There was no way I could work with him. Not after what he'd done to me. How he'd hurt me. When I opened my mouth, all that came out was "I—wh-what..."

Ryan, it seemed, did not suffer the same affliction.

"Imani, it's good to see you. Congratulations on being cast as Carmen." His smile was warm, engaging. It was the smile he'd given me a million times. The one he used to make people trust him.

Charles found the words for me. "Ryan, Imani, I'm so excited I can hardly contain myself. We're going to make the production one for the ages. Ryan, with your star power and Imani's rising star, there is no reason we can't take this production and its stars to the West End."

Panic started to overtake me. I couldn't work with him. *But you can't quit, either. This is your dream.* I'd worked hard to get there. And there was no way I was giving it up because of that asshole. I'd talk to Charles.

"Actually, Charles, if I could have a moment—"

But he had already slung an arm over each of our shoulders. "I have another surprise for you two. Since this production is such a big deal, the school has arranged for a photo shoot with the cast."

"That's great, Charles," Ryan said. Everything about his voice made my anger simmer inside. I turned slowly to face him, schooling my expression. Projecting a calm I didn't feel, I managed to keep my expression placid and cool.

The doors to the studio opened, and in walked a pretty black girl with reddish-brown braids. She laughed as she said something to someone behind her.

"Oh, here are the photographers now. I can't believe we

were able to get Xander Chase to photograph for us. A photo shoot with him normally costs more than my car."

"Who's Xander Chase?" I frowned.

Charles chuckled and tilted his head. *"That's* Xander Chase."

I tracked the direction of his chin and the gaze of every other female in the room. They were all focused on the doorway.

Behind the girl strode in the most beautiful man I'd ever seen. And he was all too familiar. His sandy-blond hair fell over his brow, and he was laughing with the girl in front of him. His smile was unfiltered and had the power to make women stare. "Oh, shit." *Alexander.*

Charles laughed. "Yeah. You would not be the first woman, or man for that matter, to say that."

"I—uh. I'm not, uh..." *Stop talking. Just stop.* There was something about the way he looked at the girl. He was totally smitten with her. A knot of pain twisted around my stomach. *Suck it up. It's not like last night was special.* As far as he was concerned, I was the worst escort known to mankind. Why was this my life? First Ryan, now this.

"Wipe the drool off your lip, darling." Ryan's voice was mocking. "Let's go meet our photographer."

Charles led the way while I tried to find a good reason for escape. My breathing accelerated as I drew nearer to him. Hot and sexy looked up with a smile, his gaze focused on my director. "Charles?" He stuck out his hand. "Good to meet you, mate." Indicating the girl, he added, "This is my assistant, Abbie Nartey."

"Pleasure." Charles tugged Ryan and I closer. There was no way to avoid it, so I went with it and stumbled forward. "These are our stars, Imani Aysem Brooks and Ryan Ellison."

I didn't dare meet Xander's gaze. Not that I could avoid it. There was no kind of manual to deal with these kinds of situations. Like, here is what to do in the instance of pretending to be an escort the night before, then running into the person the next morning. Nor did I think there was a Hallmark card for such an occasion. Cowardly as I was, I chose to shake Abbie's hand first. It was probably safer that way. The girl smiled warmly at me. "Congratulations. I hear Carmen is a great part."

I relaxed marginally. "You're American."

Abbie laughed. "It's nice to hear a familiar accent."

"It is. And thank you. We'll see if I can do the part justice." Peripherally, I could hear Ryan and Xander exchanging greetings. *Be calm. Be calm. Be calm. And shit, if you can't be calm, fake that shit till you make it.* Inwardly bracing myself, I turned my attention to Xander and offered my hand while Ryan introduced himself to Abbie.

Xander's jovial grin had morphed into a scowl. The slight cock of his head indicated confusion, and his narrowed eyes did an excellent job of communicating his anger. The intensity of his glare was enough to make my teeth lock together. Would he out me? He couldn't. At least not without outing himself too.

He glanced at my hand then back at my face, and heat prickled my skin. I sure as hell wasn't going to be intimidated, though. It wasn't as if I'd planned this. Stubbornly, I kept my hand out, daring him to shame himself by not taking it. "It's a pleasure to meet you, Xander. Charles was just telling me how lucky we are to have you both."

His scowl only deepened, and his slate-gray eyes darkened. Lips pressed into a thin line, he took my hand, and I immediately wished he hadn't. It was like holding on to a live wire, the spike of electricity was so strong.

His much larger hand enveloped mine, and his nostrils flared slightly as his pupils dilated. Despite the hostility, a flicker of awareness bloomed, and as far as my body was concerned, we were the only two people in the room. My brain did me no favors as it recalled the hot need flooding my veins as he took my nipple into his mouth, or the way he'd coaxed my orgasm out of me with his words.

My brain tried to give the command to let go of his hand or pull back. Something. Instead, we stayed locked in that position. The charged electricity tore down the walls between us, baring our souls to each other. The only word that my brain registered was *want*. Even after that mind-numbing orgasm last night. One he'd given me with very little effort on his part. The heat pooling between my thighs didn't lie. Even if I'd admonished myself a million times since running out of his flat that morning, it didn't change the fact that I responded to him in a way I didn't think I'd be able to respond to anyone ever again. What the hell was wrong with me?

And then I felt it, the stroke of his thumb over my knuckle. He might not even have realized he was doing it because his wide-eyed expression mirrored my surprise.

Jerking my hand back, I turned my attention to Abbie, who was now glaring at Xander. I tensed. *Shit.* Was I about to be at the center of some kind of lover's spat? *Stupid, stupid, stupid.* It was totally not my fault. The guy was walking sex appeal... with a penchant for hookers. Okay, maybe a little my fault. I plastered what I hoped was an appropriate *mea culpa* expression on my face.

But when Abbie turned to face me, her expression was just as warm as before. "Why don't we get you set up with lighting."

Uh, okay... Maybe they had some weird polyamorous thing going. No judgment. Except, maybe a *little* judgment. I couldn't imagine sharing someone like Xander.

After I cleared my throat and regained my composure, I said, "Sure thing," then led the way down the stairs to the stage, refusing to turn back. Even though I could feel the heat of Xander's scowl on my back.

Xander

What the fuck? I stared at my hand flexing it, then stared back up at Abbie and Imani's retreating forms. My life had just gotten a hell of a lot more complicated. I nearly vibrated with anger and residual need. I'd known the girl was no escort, but this? She'd taken a hell of a risk last night for what? A role? Research? What if I'd been some kind of nutter?

"Is there a problem?" Charles's soft question was my first clue that I was acting like I *was* a complete nutter. *Bloody fantastic.*

"Nope. Everything's wicked. Let's get started, shall we?"

"Yeah, right this way. For this shoot, we wanted to focus on the announcement of the leads. The final play each year is usually a pretty big deal. It's an even bigger deal this year because of the play and our actors. Ryan has been building a portfolio here in Britain for years now, since he was a child, so he's well-known. But Imani is a newcomer."

Ryan interjected. "Let me just say I'm a huge fan of your work. I was at your gallery opening at The Tate."

"Uh, thanks." That opening seemed like a million lifetimes ago.

"I'm excited you're going to be photographing us. Imani's pretty nervous, so if you need help getting her to cooperate, I can help with that. We're pretty close."

The note of boastfulness set my nerves on edge, and I slid Ryan a glance. But the guy wasn't looking at me. He was looking at Imani. I didn't like the proprietary way he looked at her. It was clear to anyone that this moron wanted her. And that knowledge was enough to nearly blind me with rage. *Mine.* I'd been the one making her come last night. Just the mention of her name was enough to set my teeth on edge, and I clamped my jaw together. Fuck, I really needed to get a grip. *Get your shit together.*

Charles continued. "Obviously Imani's American, one of the few in the program, and for all intents and purposes, she's the star. So it's really her debut, and we want to make it as splashy as possible. Shane McQueen is the writer, and it's an adaptation of her novel from two years ago."

I remembered the one. It was a gritty tale of a woman's journey from the back-alley streets of Soho where her mother had been a prostitute to Fleet Street and the love she had to give up to get there. It had won a slew of awards both here and across the pond, and it sat at the top of the charts for months. McQueen had said that she would never sell the rights for a film but would support producing it for the stage. For RADA to have it was a huge coup, especially since it could have easily opened on the West End or on Broadway.

I had a hard time accepting that a little slip of a girl like Imani could carry a role like that. "Is she any good?"

Charles grinned. "She's amazing. And the best part is

she has no idea. She embodies both the ingénue and the vamp. It's why the selection committee chose her to attend here. Imani slips in and out of characters so easily, like she's putting on a pretty frock. No matter how ugly the role is, she attacks it. You believe she *is* the character. You should come to the opening. I'll secure you tickets."

Bollocks to that. There was no way I was sitting through a performance by that girl. Especially since I already knew how soft she was. My cock begged to differ as my erection strained against my jeans. I'd likely have a permanent imprint of my zipper.

Maybe it was possible for Abbie to do this one on her own. She'd been working with me for months now, and she was good. *Very* good. Anything to avoid being this close to Imani. *Coward.*

In the distance, she and Abbie laughed over something, and it felt like I was punched in the gut. My gaze flickered to Abbie first, but it was Imani that held it. With an animated smile on her face and her eyes lit with humor, she was stunning to look at.

Easy does it. I sucked in a deep breath and tried to steady myself, but my brain conjured up scenarios I didn't need. I already knew how she kissed, how soft her skin was, what her pussy felt like milking my fingers. The part of my brain I normally kept under lock and key conjured up darker images that made me tight and itchy. Like that wide sexy mouth and what would it look like wrapped around my—

"I'll just help Abbie get set up, then we'll be on our way." I unpacked my camera and attached the strap to keep my hands busy. Excusing myself, I started with the lighting set up. Normally Abbie would do it on her own, but I needed something more to do with my hands.

From the corner of my eye, I watched as Charles had Ryan and Imani take their marks. Imani recited several of her lines, and I stared. Hell, everyone stared. It was just a couple of lines, but for that moment, she commanded everyone around her.

Abbie's voice broke my reverie. "You want to tell me who shoved that stick up your ass?"

I cocked my head. "I'm British, this is just how I am. No stick up the ass required."

"Don't be daft, Xander. I know when something is going on with you. You want to tell me why you're being such a douche to that poor girl?"

She always knew when something was going on with me, and I didn't like it. She was privy to information about my past that I would rather not have her know. "I'm not being arsey. I'm just getting ready to work."

"As your brother would say, bollocks. What's going on?"

I ground my teeth together. What the hell did she know? "Everything is fine. Let's just get to work."

She spread her arms. "I came ready to work. You're the one acting all crazy. Sniping at that girl."

"Fucking drop it, Abbie. You are *my* assistant. Act like it."

She blinked at me in surprise, then threw her hands up. "It's your show. Like always. But try to keep in mind that this is my career too. I'm hitched to you like an unwanted albatross. So your damage is my damage."

I could see the hurt in her eyes, and I wanted to make it better, to soothe the lash, but I couldn't seem to contain the anger ricocheting inside me.

I snatched up my favorite Nikon and left Abbie to finish the lighting. I didn't need the shrink lesson from her. Not right now. I had work to do.

CHAPTER EIGHT

IMANI

I placed my hands against the brick in the courtyard and sucked in several deep breaths. What the fuck was I going to do? I would give a million dollars to start the day all over again. As it was, I was already in the hole a couple of grand. What was a million more?

"Think, Imani, think. There is a way out of this mess. You just have to find it." One problem at a time. Of my current stink piles, Ryan was the most pressing. I had to talk to Charles—alone. And pronto. For the last two years, I'd been trying to bury the memories of my first year in London. I'd worked my ass off to get back to normal. No way was I going back to being that girl. "Are you out here hiding from me or from our new photographer?"

Hearing Ryan behind me, I whirled around with my hands up. When in doubt, go for bravado. I tilted my chin up. "Maybe you've forgotten how this works. You stay the fuck away from me, you don't touch me, you don't speak to me, you don't even so much as look at me, and you get to keep your nutsack. I can't imagine that is hard for you to remember. What the fuck are you doing here? You must have known I had the lead."

His smile was slight but practiced. "Charles called, and it was a good part. You can't expect me to not take a job that would be good for my career."

I shook my head. "I should have known all those pleas for forgiveness were total bullshit. You gave me your word, but here you still are."

He ran his hands through his hair. "Look, what happened between us was... regrettable. But I don't know how long you expect me to pay penance for it. I fucked up. I know it. I've said I'm sorry. I've given you space to heal or forget or whatever. But I need to work. If you don't want to be near me, then you can quit."

Anger coursed through me, making me vibrate. "Regrettable? Did you just fucking say regrettable? You *know* what you did to me. You knew the second you did it. That's why you showed up at my flat the next day crying like a baby, begging for *my* forgiveness. And you thought I would just conveniently forget? That it's been two whole years, so I wouldn't remember?" I stared him down, daring him to refute my words, and he had the good sense to slide his gaze away. "What you did..." My voice broke and trailed off. How dare he stroll back into my life and think I would have no problem with him?

"I'm sorry, Imani. I never meant to hurt you. But it's been long enough. You can't punish me forever."

I dug into a well of strength I wasn't sure I had, but I wasn't letting him get away with this like he had before. I was not the same girl, alone and ashamed and willing to accept my culpability. "Why don't we call a spade a spade, Ryan? You *raped* me. I loved you, and you raped me."

He flinched backward as if I'd physically slapped him. "You know it wasn't like that. You act like I was some stranger who dragged you off the street and assaulted you."

"You *did* assault me, you piece of shit. I said no."

He took a step toward me, and I immediately took one back. "I'm not going to hurt you. Jesus, Imani. We had been drinking. And you—you were looking so beautiful, and you were my girlfriend. And you wanted me. I know you did. It wasn't like I was trying to hurt you. I just wanted to be close to you. I never—Fuck. I didn't know you were a virgin. I thought you were messing me about."

Hearing those words from him was like having a bucket of ice poured over me. "What part didn't you understand, asshole? When I said no? Or the part where I begged you to stop? Or the part where I said that you were hurting me? Or maybe it was the part where I was crying uncontrollably as you kept going?"

He tightened his jaw. "You need to know I'm not that

person. If I'd known, I never would have—" He inhaled deeply. "You were my *girlfriend*. It wasn't like you said. I'm not a monster, for fuck's sake. I loved you. I *still* care about you. But I can't have you saying these things about me."

"So what? You plan on shutting me up somehow? You've already done the worst thing you can to me."

"No. I just want to make sure we can work together. That's all. I wouldn't hurt you."

I raised a brow. "You'll forgive me if I don't believe you. As for working together, you can forget about it. There is no way in hell." I tried to brush past him, but he reached out and snagged my upper arm.

"Imani—"

A voice from the auditorium door interrupted Ryan. "Ellison, I'll be needing our star now."

The ice in Xander's voice chilled me to the bone. How much had he heard? Ryan's grip tightened for a moment, then he released me. "We were just catching up on old times." His voice dripped with venom, and he glared at Xander.

Xander leaned into the open doorway, his camera slung around his neck. He looked entirely relaxed, but there was something in the way he narrowed his gaze at Ryan that told me he was anything but. Ryan shoved past us, leaving us in the doorway.

We all stood like that as if in a silent play. But finally, Ryan exited through the main entrance. Even with him gone, I didn't relax. "I guess you're ready for me?" I asked him quietly.

Xander nodded slowly. "If you're done making out with your boyfriend, I'll need you on stage."

I flinched as I thought about how we must have looked. "Not your business."

His voice low, he said, "Even after what happened between us last night? Tell me, can he make you come like I did last night?"

I scowled at him.

"I'll take that as a no. Just tell me, what are you doing with that cunt?"

Did he really think I wanted to be there with Ryan? To have his hands all over me? I spoke through clenched teeth. "Screw you."

Xander smirked. "Does last night count? Because I feel like we've already done that."

In that moment, I wasn't sure who I hated more, Ryan or Xander. As I walked toward the stage, I heard a voice behind me. "He's kind of an ass sometimes. But I promise you, he has some redeeming qualities. You just have to find them."

I glanced up when Abbie joined me in the aisle. "I assume you mean Xander. And if that's the case, I'm going to have to take your word for it."

"I wasn't the biggest fan of his when I met him either,

but he grows on you." The other girl nodded reassuringly. "Like a fungus."

Despite the morning I was having, I laughed. "Thanks. I was sort of in need of that."

"Anytime. His heart's mostly in the right place. He can just be an ass sometimes."

"I don't know how you manage to work with him."

"Between the women literally running over me to throw themselves at him, to the assitude we just discussed, I expect canonization any day now." I wondered if I'd gotten it wrong. Maybe the two of them weren't a thing. Or at the very least, as far as Abbie was concerned.

"You've got my vote." We climbed the stairs to the stage. "Where do you want me?"

"We'll start with you on the Fleet Street set first, over here. If you don't mind, let's sit you on the edge of the desk." Set design had been working for months already, so luckily some of the sets were already in working order.

"Sure thing."

While Abbie arranged me, she whispered. "Look, I know you don't know me, but I have to ask, mostly because I wish someone had asked me. Are you okay? You know, with Ryan. I wasn't spying or anything, but I saw how he grabbed you in the courtyard."

Heat suffused my face. "Great, did everyone see?"

Abbie shook her head. "No. I was about to come out

there when Xander stepped in. I just know what it's like to need someone to ask me if I was okay."

"Truth?"

My new friend nodded.

"Probably not. But I will be."

"Okay, but uh, if you need someone to talk to, I'm around. I know what it's like to date, or to have once dated, the wrong guy."

I rapidly blinked the tears out of my eyes. I had a hard time believing this confident girl had once been like me. "Ryan was a mistake I made a long time ago. Never to be repeated."

Abbie nodded. "Glad to hear it. Offer stands anyway."

Where was this girl two years ago when I was desperate for someone to talk to? "Thanks. I appreciate it."

"Listen, if you want, some of us are headed out tonight. You should come. You look like you could use some fun to take your mind off today."

Fun. That hadn't been part of my vocabulary for a while. I still had to figure out how to help Ebony. But a night out wouldn't kill me. Maybe if I were less stressed, I'd come up with a better solution to my problem. "That actually sounds like a good idea."

CHAPTER NINE

XANDER

The last place on Earth I wanted to be was at this club tonight. From start to finish, the whole fucking day had been shite. Not entirely true. It had started well with Imani in my arms, but from there it went completely downhill.

I'd started out the day desperate to have her. But then she'd vanished on me. Only to resurface in the one place I didn't need her. Complete with a twat of a boyfriend. *Fuck*. This shite would only happen to me.

I hadn't meant to act like a total arse, but seeing her there had thrown me for a loop. All I wanted was a chance to have a private conversation with her. But I'd had a job to do. And Abbie hadn't really left my side for most of the shoot. No real time to say, *Hey, about last night. You know when you pretended to be a hooker and gave me the hottest orgasm I've had in years. I'd like a repeat.*

And by the time I'd finished with the rest of the cast she was long gone. I was still holding out hope for Miriam, but she hadn't texted or called me back all day.

At least I knew where to find her, though Charles had said proper rehearsals wouldn't start for another two weeks. So the timing was bad. I needed her help in less than a week.

The music blared, the latest hip-hop track mashed up with house music underlying it. All of Alexi's friends had come out to congratulate the happy couple. The idea that my little brother was getting married still seemed insane to me. When had he grown up?

"You look like you are in need of another drink."

It was hard not to smile at the infectious blonde with the bubbly personality and the Geordie accent. Faith was one of Abbie's best friends and spent a good deal of time at the studio, in particular when there were male models being shot. "Thanks, Faith, but I've probably had enough."

"At my count, two is hardly enough to celebrate with. You at least need another. Come on, try a screaming orgasm with me," she said with a wink.

My brows shot up. Was she flirting with me? It was always hard for me to tell these days.

"Oh, Faith, leave the poor man alone." Sophie, another

friend of Abbie's, slid between us. "He needs to work up a thirst first; let's go dance."

Sophie slid her hand into mine and tugged me to the center of the VIP section. I wasn't in the mood, but for Lex and Abbie, I could put on a brave face. I snuck a glance in their direction and the smile on my brother's face as he watched his fiancée said it all. He was a completely blissed-out twat, and it couldn't have happened to a better man. *Certainly not you.*

Sophie was fun and enthusiastic. She also had a way of attracting attention. Before I knew it, several blokes were dancing on the periphery, trying to get her to dance with them. *Suckers.* She might dance like a free woman, but her boyfriend, Max, was never far away.

The DJ changed the music again to something groovier, and I leaned into her. "I'm going to head out for some fresh air. I'll see you back at the table." She nodded and waved at me.

What I wanted to do was make my escape. But that wasn't fair to Lex or Abbie. I could suck it up for an hour or two. I sidled up to the bar, signaling for the bartender. If I was going to stay, there was no reason I had to do it sober. To my right, a curvy brunette looked me up and down.

"I was wondering if you were ever going to come over and talk to me," she said with a sly smile.

She wasn't my usual type. Who was I kidding? Most of

the time, I didn't have a type beyond beautiful. And I could find something beautiful about nearly every woman I came across. At the same time, she was brasher than I liked. "Well, a beautiful woman like you doesn't strike me as the type to sit around and wait to be hit on. You seem like a go-getter."

She grinned. "So, you were waiting for me to come and get you then?"

Under normal circumstances, I'd be all about this woman. She was beautiful, available, and didn't require much work. Best of all, she wouldn't require a repeat performance. But somehow, I couldn't stir up much interest. *This is what you need. Maybe last night wasn't a fluke.* But even as the thought ran through my skull, I knew that was a lie. I could do the easy thing, go home with this girl, revel in her curves, try to forget. But I wouldn't. I couldn't. Because unlike last night, I felt absolutely zero connection to this girl. She wasn't Imani.

"Tonight, I'm just here to drink."

Full of confidence, she pressed up against me. She reached out and palmed my semi-erect cock, forcing a choke out of me. "You're sure that's all you want to do?"

Without knowing what I was looking for, I searched the crowd. The hairs on the back of my neck stood at attention. It was then that I saw her. *Imani.* She grinned, waving at Abbie, who stood and hugged her. I could only stare in shock as Abbie introduced her around and my brother kissed her on the cheek. *Traitor.* What the hell was she doing here?

I removed the curvy brunette's hand from my groin. "Sorry, love, but like I said, not tonight." My instincts didn't bother to engage my brain in the conversation. I couldn't have walked in the opposite direction if I tried. When I reached her, she looked up and gave a startled jump.

"Karma really is a bitch. Seriously, why can't I escape you?"

I grinned. "You must have done something very naughty in a past life. Or maybe just last night. You're crashing my brother's party."

She cocked her head. "You should probably look up the definition of crashing. I was invited by Abbie."

"You and I never got a chance to talk. You know, because you ran out on me."

She flicked her dark hair over her shoulder and licked her bottom lip. "What's there to talk about?"

"You mean, besides how we met last night? Or what you look like when you come with my name on your lips? Or how I've come to know about that cute little mole on your left breast. Or maybe how your puss—"

Her eyes went wide. "Would you shut up before somebody hears you?" Her gaze skittered around.

She was way too easy to rile up.

She slid her gaze back to me as she lowered her voice.

"Look, I would rather no one find out about..." She waved her left hand. "You know."

I feigned ignorance. "Oh, you mean the whole escort thing."

"Shut. Up," she muttered through clenched teeth as she put her hand on my chest and shoved. I didn't budge, but the heat of her palm seared my chest.

"Relax. Jesus, thank God you weren't nearly this uptight last night. All I need is ten minutes. Hear me out, then you never have to talk to me again."

"I seriously want to forget that last night ever happened. I was an idiot. I know it. I don't understand why you won't just be like every normal guy I know and avoid me like the plague."

Because right now, you're the only one who can make me come. "Follow me."

She followed willingly enough as I tugged her through the crowd and up the stairs to the rooftop. Even though it was only April, the weather was balmy and warm. And despite the fact that we were on a rooftop in the middle of London, it was as though we'd been transported to a lush greenhouse. This was the best feature of the club in my opinion. I loved it up there so much I often chose it for shoots.

She stared in awe at all the flowers and touched several delicate petals. "What am I doing up here, Xander?"

"Better question, why were *you* in my flat last night?"

She tipped her chin up to meet my gaze. "I'm not a whore."

The air whooshed out of my lungs, and my head snapped back as if she'd physically slapped me. "I fucking know that. What did you think? I was chasing you down to make sure you took your money? What is it you Yanks would call me? Captain Save-a-ho? Not fucking likely. I'm no one's savior. I've dealt with a lot of escorts in my life, and I knew from the moment I touched you, you weren't one."

Her bottom lip trembled. "Then what do you want from me?"

I took three steps until I stood directly in front of her. With every exhale, I could feel her warm breath on my cheeks. "For starters, I want you to tell me what you were doing there. We've established you're not a whore. That makes what you were doing even riskier. I think we can both agree that meeting some strange bloke at his flat for 'talking' is a huge lapse in judgment."

She lifted a brow. "Really, you want to do this?"

I crossed my arms. There was nothing I liked more than when her eyes sparked with fire.

She sighed. "At first it was for the role. Research. But then, I was fucking desperate. Miriam made it sound too good to be true. And so easy. All I had to do was show up and talk to you and I could get the money I needed." She puffed out a breath. "Well, you know what happened next."

"Why didn't you take the money? You said you needed it."

"In the morning..." Her voice trailed off as she shook her head. "I didn't like how I felt. I wasn't *that* desperate." She shook her head. "And what happened. I didn't plan it —it wasn't like that." Then she added a question of her own. "Why do you see hookers? You, ah, obviously don't need to."

If she only knew. "I don't pay escorts for *sex*."

She frowned as she peered back up at me. "Then why?"

"Because they're less judgmental than shrinks."

Her laugh was humorless. "And I thought I was fucked up."

"Here's the secret, sweetheart. *Everyone* is fucked up." Something in her expression was soft, vulnerable. I lifted fingers to her cheek and traced softly. "What is it about you that makes me feel like this?"

She blinked in confusion. "I'm not doing anything. I don't know how I'm making you feel."

I traced a thumb over her cheekbone. "You know. You feel it too."

She ducked her head. "Are we done?"

I licked my lips and let her go. "Not yet. I have a proposition for you."

"You know they've already done an *Indecent Proposal* movie, right? It's a classic."

Despite myself, I smirked. "Just hear me out. I need someone to go to Paris with me for four days."

Her brows rose. "See earlier comment about me not being a whore." She took a deliberate step away from me. "You know, you're very good. You almost had me believing that bit about how I made you feel. But let me say it again and this time do try to listen. I. Am. Not. A. Whore. You are not Richard Gere, and clearly, I am no Julia Roberts. You don't get a girlfriend experience."

"I need someone to *pose* as my girlfriend for four days. I'm not expecting anything in return. No sex. Just hang on my arm, socialize. Make me look good. I'll pay you five thousand pounds." I held up my hands and pressed on when she frowned. "Think of it as an acting job. Plain and simple."

She narrowed her gaze. "Who would I be pretending for?"

"The board and president of the London Artistic Trust. I need to appear settled and reformed from my bad-boy ways. It's very important that I make it onto this board."

"Why?"

No way I was going into that now. "It's complicated, but trust me, it's important. Life and death important."

She shook her head. "Look, I don't think—"

"I'm desperate. I'm willing to beg."

Imani's gaze slid around the roof as she started to pace.

"But you have Miriam. You could take her. She's used to playing the girlfriend."

She has a point, you git. "I know, but for better or worse, the chemistry with us is real. Palpable. Any idiot can see it. It'll help sell it to LeClerc. Secondly, you seem to need the money. It's a win-win. And I'll keep my hands to myself. You'll be perfectly safe with me."

She scoffed. "As if. Why can't you take Abbie?"

I laughed. "Well, since she's about to become my sister-in-law, that will hardly make it look like I'm a *reformed* bad boy." Frustrated, I ran my hands through my hair. "I can call Miriam, but I'd rather see that money go to you."

A slight frown creased her forehead. "Sister-in-law? Seriously?" She shook her head. "You don't even know me."

She had a point there. "Truth?"

She nodded.

"You're the first person I've connected to in so long I can't even remember."

"I thought you said this wasn't about sex."

"It's not." I started to sweat. "It's more about someone who understands me. Paris will be a test of improv skills. There are a few people who don't want me on the board, and they will do anything to make sure that doesn't happen. You're quick on your feet. You have a smart mouth. And I promise you, if we sleep together, it'll have nothing to do with the money."

Her eyes went wide as she studied me while crossing her arms. "Are you planning on trying anything?"

I wisely bit back a laugh. "Well, I'm a bloke. So, of course, I'll think about touching you again. But those are errant thoughts; my focus is this job. I need *you* to pull it off. So that will be my focus, not getting you wet and writhing underneath me again."

Imani rolled her lips in. As if she were holding back her words. "I see you're not taking it off the table."

I let my gaze slide over her magnificent cheekbones and the smooth skin of her neck to her delicate collarbone, then dropped it lower to her breasts. No, I was certainly not taking it off the table. I licked my lips. "How about we call me a pragmatist. You and I clearly have some chemistry, so there's really no point in denying it. Besides, what happens in Paris stays in Paris."

"There won't be anything happening in Paris."

"You sound confident in that."

"That's because I am. The other night won't be happening again."

"Understood." I should probably have warned her there was nothing I loved more than a challenge.

CHAPTER TEN

XANDER

"A lexander, you have to stop this campaign against Alistair."

I pinched the bridge of my nose as I pulled into a parking spot at Heathrow. Damn my brother for telling her what we were up to. "Hello to you too, Mother." I loved my mother. But our relationship was complicated. Whenever she called, the overwhelming emotion was guilt. For the both of us. She, because she still felt responsible for what had happened. And I, because I could never seem to let it go and give her the absolution she craved.

She sighed. "Alexander—"

"Mum," I interrupted. "You realize you're not going to talk me out of anything. It's already in motion."

"You know how much I love you. My request has less

to do with Alistair than it has to do with you. We need to put all of that behind us and move on."

Move on. "Maybe that was easy for you to do, Mother. But not for me. I can't move on. I wake up every day and my first thoughts are about Silas and Alistair and what they've done. *You* might have been able to walk away from their sins unscathed, but I haven't been able to shed it as quickly."

"Why do you think that I walked away from it? There isn't a day I don't think about you or your brother. I have to live with the fact that I failed you and Alexi every day. I wish I had known, wish I had seen. Wish I hadn't been blind. I wish I'd been the one to take that man's life. But what you're doing—you're only picking at the scab. Making it bleed unnecessarily. What do you need from me to stop this?"

Through clenched teeth I muttered, "I don't need you to say anything. I've never needed you to say anything." I just wanted this to be over. And this was the way I saw to end it.

"I could tell you until I'm blue in the face how worried I am. I failed you. I know that. But you have to stop. If you want to punish someone, punish me."

I'd gotten over the anger at my mother years ago. I wasn't angry with her anymore. Alistair, on the other hand, would not be so lucky. "Mum, I'm not trying to punish you, I swear." I followed the signs to the private airstrip. "This is something I have to do. I wish it didn't hurt you, but it's important to me. It has to be done. Alistair made it a point to destroy my life. And he's benefiting from his father's work. I can't let that stand."

Deep down, I knew I was wasting my breath. She would never understand. And I would never deliberately hurt her by telling her exactly why I hated Alistair so much. As far as she was concerned, I hated Alistair simply because he was a McMahon. I didn't have the heart to tell her it was so much more than that. It would destroy her if she knew. She'd been devastated when she eventually found out about the abuse by Silas, and I would rather not do that to her again. No. This vendetta was mine. "Mum, I promise, I'm not trying to make your life more difficult. And I'll leave your name out of it. But I have to do this. I wish I could explain, but I can't."

"Look, I think you're long overdue for a visit home. Or even better, you, Alexi and I can take a holiday, just us. Reconnect."

I found it funny how she'd left my father out of the mix. The old man and Lex could barely stand to be in the same room together, so a happy family vacation was out of the question. "Mum, I'm leaving for a trip. But I'll call you when I get back. We'll have dinner."

She sighed. "There's no changing your mind, is there?"

"You know me better than that by now." At the end of this weekend I'd have Alistair exactly where I wanted him.

CHAPTER ELEVEN

IMANI

aris. It was official; I was crazy for real. Fe thought so. I might not have been exactly forthcoming about how I met Xander. Or what I was doing on this getaway for the long weekend. But I'd go and come back with nearly all of what I needed for Ebony. It was only four days. In Paris of all places. Didn't mean this whole plan wasn't shit-balls crazy. It was one thing to pretend to be an escort for a night. It was another to have to pull off a lie under scrutiny for four days.

"All right?"

I brought my head up to glance at Xander. His slate-gray eyes regarded me closely. And I was mesmerized. Framed by thick, dark, sooty lashes, they focused on me with such intensity. He had this way of looking at everything as if he wanted to see into its soul. Granted, he was a photographer, so that made sense. He had to capture emotion from all sorts of things. "You're staring."

He shrugged then sat back against his seat as our car whizzed toward Paris. "You're beautiful. I'm sure you're accustomed to it."

I rubbed the end of my nose. "No, actually. People don't usually stare at me."

"Then they're blind."

"If you say so."

The corner of his lips tipped up. "You'd think you'd believe me since I photograph beautiful things for a living."

Shifting uncomfortably in my seat, I changed the subject. "We should probably go over the cover story again."

The corner of his lips twisted into that smirk I found so sexy. "Do you study all your roles like this?"

"I want this to be my profession, so yes. I live, breathe, and eat my roles. It's how I met Miriam. I'd asked Charles if he could put me in touch with an actual escort for research purposes. I made it a point not to ask him how he'd found her."

Xander's laugh filled the car. When he smiled or laughed it completely transformed his face, making him look younger, less intense, and more mischievous. "I imagine he found her the old-fashioned way."

"Doubt it since he's gay." I shrugged. "So to be clear,

the main two people we have to convince are Jean LeClerc and Alistair McMahon."

Xander nodded. "The one to worry about is Alistair. He's actively trying to keep me off the board."

"And you're not going to tell me why?" He shook his head, but I pressed a little harder. "Knowing could help me do my job better."

"You don't need to know why."

"Fine. How much of a problem is he going to be?"

"A big one. He only has one vote out of ten, but he has sway. And stay away from him unless I'm with you." There was something about the way the muscle in his jaw worked that told me he was deadly serious.

Way to add more pressure. "Understood." I tapped the folder. "I know this folder backward and forward. How well do you know it?"

"I've been planning this for a long time. I know every detail of that folder."

I raised a brow. "How long have we been dating?"

Xander answered smoothly "Nine months."

"I'm starting you off easy, hotshot. How did we meet?"

He gave me one of his patented half smiles. "I went to meet a friend, who was a no-show. You were there instead."

I flushed, but deliberately held his gaze. "Not bad. Do you see this relationship as long term?"

Xander's gaze never left my face, but I saw a shadow cross over his expression ever so briefly. "Yes."

I wrinkled my nose. "You're going to have to do something to sell it, Xander. Otherwise you're wasting your time taking me with you. You need to make *me* believe." I cleared my throat. This was what I did best. Sliding my hand into Xander's, I focused on him and smiled. "We're in love. I can't remember my life before you walked into it with your over-confident attitude. But underneath that is a vulnerable man I can love, talk to."

Xander's lips parted and he looked like he wanted to say something, but I paused him with fingertips against his lips. "I can't imagine going a day without your touch." Against my fingertips, I could feel the slight suction as he inhaled sharply.

Xander coughed and removed my fingers from his lips. "Well, fuck. You *are* an actress. You'll make this easy." His silvery gaze drifted to my lips. "You're very good."

"Thank you. I think about it more like telling the truth of the character rather than I'm making it up as I go along. It helps."

"You can almost make me believe, and *that* is a feat." He rubbed the tip of his nose with his knuckle. "There is one more thing."

"What's that?"

"You'll be photographed with me. It could show up in a tabloid or two."

"Excuse me?" No one said anything about this being public fodder for tabloids.

"Easy now, love. I can't control them. I'm in the public eye because of my family, and let's face it, I've cultivated something of a reputation. They'll be curious about you, so you might be photographed. I'll try to keep it to a minimum."

"How long are they going to be photographing me?"

"Probably while we're in Paris. Then when we get back, they might try to catch a glimpse of you. But if you just go about your day, they'll see there's nothing interesting going on. Then a couple of weeks after I get the job, we'll stage a public breakup. They'll pretty much vanish after that. Unless of course you start dating your costar right after that."

My body went rigid, as if I'd been volunteered for the ice bucket challenge. *He doesn't know how you feel about Ryan or why. Let it go.* "That won't be happening."

He was more astute than I gave him credit for, though, and he studied me closely. "You don't like him? And given your posture, you have good cause not to like him." He cocked his head. "Care to tell me what that is?"

I pinned him with resting bitch face number one. The one that said *Back off.* "Are we about to start sharing our deepest and darkest? You want to tell me why you hate Alistair McMahon?"

Those perfect lips of his flattened into a thin line. "Fair enough."

Something tickled my memory banks. "Wait, last year I

remember some big splash about some royal cousin or something in trouble for cheating on his girlfriend. Chase something. Was that you? I remember the papers last year. Is that what it's going to be like?"

Xander shook his head. "That was my brother, Alexi. The only reason that was even a problem was because of who they thought he was engaged to at the time. It won't be like that, I promise."

"I'm having a hard time believing you. I don't want my life disrupted over this."

"And it won't be—you have my word. This will all be over in a couple of weeks."

"Somehow you're not inspiring confidence."

"Remember, from the moment we arrive, unless you're in your bedroom or the loo, assume that everyone is watching and cataloging your every move, so we have to be on. Can you do this?"

"I can do anything for a few days. I'm ready for this if you are." I forced a smile I didn't entirely feel. It was only four days. I'd survive.

⚓ ⚓

Xander

The rest of car ride through Paris, I did my best not to fidget. It didn't help that I could smell Imani's perfume. I honestly couldn't believe she'd agreed to this madness.

After all these years, I was close to finally putting this shit to bed once and for all. Next to me, Imani stared out the window, eyes wide. She might as well have been oohing and aahing for all her wonder. "I take it you've never been to Paris before."

She shook her head. "Fe, my best friend, and I were supposed to go last term, but I got an audition so we had to cancel, then work and stuff. But it's top of my list. Do you think I'll get a chance to sneak away for a couple of hours sometime this weekend? To explore a little?"

Why hadn't it even occurred to me that she would want to see Paris? "Sure. If you want, I can take you around. I'm very familiar with the city. I actually have an apartment I use in the 7th Arrondissement right across from the Eiffel Tower. I would have suggested we stay there, but I think LeClerc and Alistair want to keep an eye on me."

"You don't have to do that. I know this is a job interview for you and I'm the required arm candy."

I placed my hand over hers and she stilled, her eyes pinning to our fingers. Very deliberately, I wrapped my fingers around hers and squeezed lightly. "I'd like to. I never get to show anyone the city. I'm usually working with models who are either in and out or know the city as well as I do. And let's face it, the cafés would be wasted on them."

Imani chortled. "Good point, because I'm pretty sure I can eat my weight in plain chocolate right about now."

She was hungry. Damn. Only three hours with a girlfriend and I was already failing. "Why didn't you say you were hungry?"

She shrugged. "I know you're on a schedule. I figured I could eat once we got settled. Don't worry, I'm not at hangry levels yet."

I frowned. "Hangry?"

Her answering dimpled smile was completely arresting. "So hungry that you're pretty pissed off about it and might eat someone's arm to slake the hunger."

"That's bloody fantastic. Note to self, keep you well fed."

"We'll have you slanging like a Yank in no time."

The car pulled into a loose gravel driveway surrounded by seven- to eight-foot hedges. We drove for another full minute before the chateau came into view.

Imani's gasp was audible. "This looks like something out of a Dumas novel."

We were met by a butler wearing a tuxedo at the front stairs. "Good afternoon, Monsieur Chase. Mademoiselle. *Bienvenue* à Chateau Millieux. Gerard will show you to your room, and your bags will be brought up shortly." His French was perfectly accented, but when he spoke English, it was apparent he was British.

I knew I should be focused on the job at hand, but I kept paying attention to Imani's reactions. Something as simple as the floor fascinated her. Polished white marble lay at our feet. Priceless art hung on the walls leading to the grand staircase.

"I think I should have brought my roller skates," she muttered in a hushed tone.

"You have your own set of skates?"

"I'd better, since I'm a derby girl."

I wasn't sure what that was, but my mind, ever helpful, conjured up every dirty connotation it could dream up. "Dare I ask what a derby girl is?"

"If I'm to stay your girlfriend, we're going to have to do a crash course in all things American and fun."

Our room was on the top floor of the four-story chateau on the south side, so the lighting was beautiful. The furnishings were opulent. A beautiful four-poster bed dominated the space, despite the grand size of the room.

Imani's gaze flickered to mine. *One bed.*

Another reason why I would have preferred to stay at my own place in the city and commuted out. "Don't worry. I'll take the couch."

Imani narrowed her gaze on the settee. "No dice. You're a lot bigger than I am. Take the bed."

There was no way. I might be a prat, but I was gentleman enough to give it to her. "Not going to happen. But if you like, we can share."

Her gaze flickered to the bed, then back at me. "Not gonna happen."

"Then it's settled, you will take the bed."

My gaze focused in on her full lips as her tongue peeked out to moisturize them. "Can I ask you a question?"

"Could I stop you from asking?" The last thing I needed was her attempting to probe into my personal life... again.

"Probably not, but I suppose you could not answer."

I dragged off my tie and unbuttoned the top button of my shirt. "Then go ahead."

"Why didn't you bring a real girlfriend to this interview?"

Because I would have wanted to keep someone I cared about as far away from this shit as possible. Alistair was toxic. And I had to be just as ugly to do what I needed to do. But I couldn't say that. "It's simpler, easier, more detached. Bring a woman to Paris and all of a sudden she starts to get ideas."

She scoffed and fingered the gossamer window hangings. "You're a real romantic, aren't you?"

I grinned.

She rolled her eyes. "I think we're due downstairs."

CHAPTER TWELVE

IMANI

O f all the ideas I'd ever had in my life, this was probably not one of my best ones. I was playing a part. I just had to remember that. None of this was real. Smoke and mirrors. Then why was I letting him touch me? *Because you're pretending to be his girlfriend, idiot. Touching is part of the deal.*

I really had to start thinking through my plans better. It had seemed like such a good idea to slip my hand into his before coming down for cocktails. A fantastic idea, really. It was innocuous enough but was something real couples did. Or so I remembered from my old life when I'd had relationships. But then as soon as the doors had opened, there had been people in the hallway.

Xander had probably taken his cue from me, but the kiss he'd planted on my shoulder didn't feel like an act. It felt... *real*. At least the shivers it gave me were real. The stubble on his cheek had tickled my skin as his lips had slowly glided over me. Xander Chase was walking sin. And he very well knew it. It was in the confidence of the way he walked. The tilt of his head as he talked to women. He was aware of how good-looking he was and used it to his full advantage.

As he introduced me around, he was mildly flirtatious but never overboard, always deferring to me like a boyfriend would. Always keeping me within two feet of touching distance. As we traversed the white marble from the foyer, he gently guided me with a hand on my lower back. But every single touch, caress, and glide brought the lick of heat with it. It was making me half mad with lust. When I slanted him a glance, he blinked at me innocently.

Damn him, he knew he was driving me crazy. And this was why I hadn't wanted to do this. Because of this feeling. Every time he touched me I was transported right back to that flat in Notting Hill where a total stranger had touched me and for once made me feel something.

It didn't help things that he was smart. He floated easily from conversations about politics, to art, to current events. And of course he spoke flawless French, along with Italian and what sounded like some German. He was officially a Venus flytrap. Everything about him was meant to entice, to entwine, to ensnare.

After an hour or so of mingling, I started chatting with

a girl who worked in the marketing department. It took Xander less than twenty seconds to come looking for me. He stalked toward me like a man who knew what he wanted. Like I was his target. His prey. "Sorry to interrupt, beautiful." This time, he kissed me on the neck, lingering long enough to nuzzle. My head spun and I flushed.

The poor girl I'd been talking to shifted on her feet and tried to look anywhere but at us. "I thought this weekend wasn't about sex," I muttered, keeping my voice low.

"I'm pretty sure I told you I'd still have a go, right?"

"Not going to happen."

"If you say so." His voice was low when he spoke. "Sorry to interrupt, darling. But there's someone I want you to meet. He's the man who made all of this possible."

Ah, code words. I needed to go play nice with the douchebag who was blocking him from his job. Excusing myself from the conversation with my new friend, I let Xander lead me away.

All it took was one look and I hated Alistair McMahon on sight. It could have been his pale, gaunt looks, or what little I already knew about him. Or maybe it was the mask of disdain he wore when he saw Xander. He looked every bit the picture of refinement, but his eyes were cold, and his thin lips looked as if he never smiled. All in all, a miserable-looking man, despite his fancy suit and overall polish.

"You must be the young lady who has captured Xander's attention. I can see why he's taken with you."

I plastered my smile on. "Thank you for having me. It's a treat to come to Paris."

Alistair's shrewd gaze narrowed. "Why Xander, I would have thought you'd taken her to your *pied-à-terre* by now."

I squeezed Xander's hand to stop him from answering. I wasn't a fan of this Alistair douchebag. "Well, we were just talking about how we might have stayed at his flat instead, but we thought the chateau suited better. As least for a few days, then we'll switch venues, explore the city."

Alistair narrowed his gaze imperceptibly at me. "So, almost little brother, where have you been storing this American... gem?" Somehow the man made the word *gem* sound remarkably like *rodent*.

Little brother? Wait, what the fuck? I frowned, and Alistair tsked. "Xander didn't you tell her that we were practically family? If I were you, my darling, I'd wonder about what else he wasn't telling you."

Xander tugged me in close to his side and kissed me on the temple. "It was unimportant, so why bring it up?" Turning to me, he said, "Alistair's father almost married my mother when I was a child."

Maybe that was the reason for the too-thick tension. "What a small world. And now you two are going to be working together."

Alistair's gaze turned frostier. "Time will tell."

Xander clapped him on the shoulder. "Relax, Alistair.

This is all supposed to be a fun weekend, remember? I'm having fun. Aren't you?"

When Alistair slunk away, I turned my gaze to him. "Is that all part of the stuff I'm not supposed to worry about?"

"Don't worry about him. He's inconsequential. But this guy is not." He inclined his head toward the approaching behemoth of a man. "Jean. It's a pleasure to see you again. May I introduce to you to my girlfriend, Imani Brooks."

The larger man took My proffered hand and completely engulfed it in his. I could only pray I'd get it back one day. "*Enchanté.* I heard we were finally going to meet the beautiful woman we've been hearing so much about."

I'd add that one to the pile of questions I needed Xander to answer. "*Enchanté de te rencontrer.* This is a great party and the grounds are beautiful. Thank you for including me in the fun."

"Of course, my dear. My mother is British, but my father was French. This chateau has been in our family for centuries." His smile broadened. "You know, until last week, I was unaware that Xander had such a serious relationship." He leaned forward conspiratorially. "I'm sure you're aware of his former reputation."

I locked my smile into place. "I've always believed love can change a person."

Xander trailed a hand down the small of my back,

leaving a trail of fire in his wake. "Everything changed for me after I met Imani."

I met his silvery gaze, and there was a hint of sincerity in his eyes that I couldn't deny. *No. He's acting. Don't believe the hype.*

LeClerc smiled down at us from his towering height. "Sometimes love happens like that. It's enough to change you as a man."

"Tell me about it," Xander said. "My whole outlook on life has changed since meeting this creature."

"You know, my Charlotte did that for me twenty years ago. How did the two of you meet?"

I gave the story that we'd discussed. I embellished with sweeping emotions, but it worked great. LeClerc's wife, Charlotte, sidled up to us with a broad grin. "You two are a beautiful couple. I'm so glad Xander has learned how to keep his personal life out of the papers for once. There was a time that you couldn't open an *OK Magazine* without seeing his face and some emaciated model."

Xander took a sip of his champagne. "I'm a changed man."

Charlotte nodded. "I can see that." The older woman slid a sly glance up at her husband. Then back at the pair of us. "Now that I've met Imani, I can see what Alistair means."

Xander cocked his head. "Oh? What did Alistair have to say?"

Charlotte smiled sheepishly. "Sorry for the gossip. He was just wondering why you haven't snapped up this gorgeous creature and made her officially yours yet."

I flushed. I had to school my expression and bite back the wince when Xander's grip tightened on my hand. I wasn't sure if it was out of fear or if he was trying to keep me from running. Great, just what I needed—a pair of matchmakers. Xander had mentioned improv, but this was a little ridiculous. "I guess it's a matter of timing. Nine months really isn't that long. And we want to take our time, not rush into anything." I clasped Xander's hand and beamed him a smile. "All that will come one day. There's no rush. When you know, you know."

Charlotte LeClerc scoffed. "Sometimes young love has to win out," she said.

Her husband nodded. "The two of you are clearly in love. And if I'm honest with you, Charlotte and I eloped when we were young. We didn't wait."

I slid a glance at Xander, begging for help. How was I supposed to wiggle out of this one? There was no script. *Say something, dumbass. Anything.*

His gaze flickered to mine, and I watched as his Adam's apple bobbed up and down. His attention went back to the LeClercs and back to me again. "Wow, put on the spot, actually. But I've been carrying this thing about with me for ages, and I was hoping to do this in Paris this week, but you're absolutely correct. When it's right, why wait?"

Letting go of my hand, he reached up to his neck and took off the chain and ring he wore around his neck. In the light, the rose gold shone and the stones around it gleamed. He slipped the ring off the chain and dropped to one knee.

Oh God. Oh shit. No. No! This was not part of the deal.

"Imani Aysem Brooks, my life changed when I first saw you. I'd never met any woman who makes me feel the way that you do. You astonish me with your wit and your smile, and I cannot get you out of my head." He licked his lips and his voice trembled when he spoke again. "I love you. Will you marry me?"

No, hell no.

All eyes were on me, and Xander held my hand tight, his gaze imploring me to trust him. I knew without a doubt that was the last thing I should do. But still, the word that tumbled out of my mouth was, "Yes."

I. Could. Not. Breathe. It was like an out-of-body experience watching Xander slide the ring made of rose gold and emeralds onto my finger. The lighting in the ballroom hit them just so, making them shimmer.

This was supposed to be a simple one-time thing. Go to this weekend away. Pose as Xander's girlfriend. Get paid five thousand pounds. This was not supposed to happen. But no matter how I steeled myself, I was completely unprepared for what he did next.

Rising to his feet, Xander pulled me close. When he slid his hand into my hair and cupped my face, I fought the urge to flee. *What are you doing?* I mouthed.

Kissing my fiancée, he mouthed back.

I froze in an attempt to brace myself. After the other night, I'd told myself I wasn't going to go back to that feeling. While the free-fall was awesome, the landing was too hard to survive. But still, here I was, about to walk off a cliff with him... again.

He angled his head and halted just before his lips touched mine. Pressed so close against him, I could feel his heart hammering, matching the thundering beat of my own.

Our kiss in his flat had been a shocking frenzy of need. He had caught me off guard, but even more so by the raw emotion that coursed through me the moment his lips touched mine. This time was different.

Xander's lips melted over mine slowly, as if he had all the time in the world. As if we were the only two people in the room and no one was watching. His tongue took command of mine in a sensual dance, choreographed to tease. Every slow stroke of his tongue was followed by a teasing retreat. I didn't know much about this man, but I was certain of one thing. He was an expert at this. Kissing could well be a full-time job for him. It didn't matter how much I steeled myself; there was no preparing for Xander Chase.

When he pulled back, my body swayed toward him. Desperate for more of the bliss he promised me. Slowly the sound blocked out by his kiss began to filter in again. There was applause. *Lots* of applause. And when I looked around, several women were fanning themselves.

He released me and the room spun. The chiffon and satin of dresses swirled together. I needed air. Space. Distance from Xander. "If you'll excuse me for just a minute. I'm just going to get some fresh air..." On unsteady feet, I weaved my way through the throngs of guests at the party. The vibrant colors of their dresses and their ties clashing together made my head throb. The crowd finally thinned, and I stumbled onto the balcony, greedily gulping in deep breaths of fresh air. The temperature was in the mid-fifties, so not exactly warm, but the bite of the chill helped the panic recede.

The shadow of fear evaporated in the night air and I could breathe easier again. There was no way I could let that happen again. I wasn't afraid of him. He might be a total stranger, but he'd had prime opportunity to hurt me and he hadn't. What I was afraid of was my response to him and what I felt after he touched me. Out of control of my body. Needy, and desperate for something I couldn't quite name.

I'd gotten myself into this mess by trying to do everything for everyone. What I should have done was taken Fe up on his offer. Instead, my stupid pride got me in trouble.

Even as the thought filtered in, I frowned. No. I couldn't have done that, knowing the pain that money caused him. I was a big girl; I could get out of my own mess. All I had to do was tell Xander I was leaving. Leaning against the thick stone armament, I tried to quell my queasy stomach. I'd never backed down from a challenge before, but maybe there was a first time for everything.

"Imani?"

Xander's voice brought me upright and I met his steel-gray gaze. "I can't do this." I half expected him to try to convince me otherwise or talk me into it, but he just took my hand and nodded.

His voice was soft. "I'm sorry. This is my fault; I didn't see it coming. I anticipated a dozen other outcomes. Just nothing like this, so I improvised."

Bleary-eyed, I studied the ring. "Where did you get this?"

"It belonged to someone I knew."

Great, recycled love. "We can't get married. You have to un-improvise. Something. Anything. I can't marry you."

He slid his glance around before lowering his voice. "Of course we're not getting married. I was just following Charlotte's lead. Besides, fiancée looks better than girlfriend."

I touched my still tingling lips. "Xander—"

"You know, neither one of you looks like a happy married-couple-to-be. Matter of fact, Xan, your new bride looks a little green around the gills." Alistair's smile was sly, looking more like a smug smirk. "Now is that because you suddenly realized that you're about to tie yourself to a paranoid, lying reprobate or because this isn't what you bargained for? What did he promise you, a fun weekend away?"

"Leave her be, Alistair." Xander stepped in front of me, shielding me from Alistair and giving me a clear view of his back. Somewhere during the night, he'd shed his jacket, and I could see his muscles bunch under his dress shirt. He was lean but wiry, and I knew from experience how hard every single one of his muscles were. Not to mention, there was an edge to him. If it came to a fight, Alistair would lose. Which didn't bother me one bit.

What *did* bother me was that Xander might actually kill the smug asshole.

"Take your little girlfriend and go home, Xander. That kiss might have everyone else fooled, but I know you. You're not stable enough to maintain a girlfriend. Sooner or later LeClerc is going to see through your lie. You don't belong at the adults' table." He shifted his gaze to me. "Why don't you crawl back under whatever dingy rock he found you under? You don't belong here."

"Shut it, Alistair. Or you will be eating your teeth and the only thing you'll be able to swallow this weekend is the *foie gras*."

The tension swirled around them thick and opaque,

and I could almost taste it. Something else was going on here. Something I didn't understand. But one thing I did know was that Alistair was an asshole. I'd come to do a job, and I wasn't leaving until I did. And if this douche waffle got an ass-handing in the process, well, I was totally down for that.

I squared my shoulders. "Actually Alistair, Xander and I were just talking about when we could have Charlotte and Jean to our place for dinner. I love to cook, and it's finally our chance to entertain, given our schedules. Besides, I'd like to say thank you to them for inviting me along this weekend."

Alistair scowled. "Your place? You expect me to believe you two live together?"

Xander pulled me close to his side and his spicy after-shave made me want to nuzzle into him. "We've been living together for months. Given what happened with my last fiancée, I've kept this relationship under wraps."

What the hell did he mean by that? I'd ask him about it later. Standing on tiptoe, I kissed his jaw. "I'm afraid Xander has been trying to keep me all to himself. Now, if you'll excuse us, I need to call home and squeal over the news." Without giving him another glance, I slipped my hand into Xander's and tugged him toward the main entrance and the stairs leading to our suite, not letting go until we were safe from prying eyes.

Xander shut the door behind them quietly. "What did you just agree to?"

Oh boy. Wrapping my arms around my belly, I paced. "Apparently we're living together."

"Yeah, love, I gathered that much. But you don't know Alistair. He'll check. I can have the staff say you live there, but that will only last for so long. He'll use that as an opportunity to show LeClerc that I'm bullshitting him. It will actually have to be real. At least until I get myself on that board."

Fuck. I paced along the hardwood floor. "Sorry, he was just such a smug fucker I lost my mind. I don't know what your beef with him is, but what I do know is that he's not a nice person, so whatever you have planned for him, bring it on."

"Looks like you're moving in then."

CHAPTER THIRTEEN

XANDER

I clawed at the darkness, desperate to find the light. I didn't dare look back, because if I did, there would be no coming back. I had to keep moving. Had to keep fighting. Behind me, I could hear Silas's heavy breathing, panting, thundering footsteps. Icy cold hands clawed at my back as if Silas was trying to reach me from beyond the grave. And then there was the empty silence.

Somewhere ahead, an angel called for me. "Xander?"

If I could just follow the sound, I'd be safe. Happy. Warm.

Slowly the dream lifted even as I tried to make it to the mysterious angel. Slowly I blinked sleep from my eyes, and Imani was standing over me, a hand on my thigh. "Xander. Are you awake?"

With the adrenaline still coursing through my veins,

my heart worked overtime pumping blood to my body. She was so close. She smelled so good. One taste of heaven and I'd wake up. But for now, I clung to the dream, tugging her closer until she was close enough to taste.

Her lips were so soft. So sweet. Just having her near was enough to banish the darkness from my mind and I needed that. The problem was eventually the warm glow turned white-hot and my tongue licked at the seam of her lips.

She parted them on a sigh, granting me access, and I took full advantage. With a low groan, I yanked her down to me and rolled our bodies so that I lay half on top of her, blanket tangled around our legs.

Her fingers dug into my biceps as she clung to me, and my mind spun. Need coursed through my blood and my erection strained against the cotton of my pajama bottoms. She wore only a thin t-shirt and shorts, and I was shirtless; I could feel her nipples pebble where my chest met hers.

But it wasn't until her tongue slid against mine, until she kissed me back, that I lost control.

Roughly, I shifted her until my hips lay between her thighs. And I claimed her mouth, devouring it, wanting to erase any other kiss from her memory.

Beneath me, her hips rolled into mine, and my cock throbbed. The edges of my consciousness started to gray, and I felt a tingle at the base of my spine. *Fuck.* I wasn't coming in my pants again with her.

But I couldn't bear to *stop* touching her, not yet. *Just a little bit longer.* I'd hold on to heaven before I returned to hell where I belonged. With one hand I gripped her hip, stilling her movements. The other fisted in her hair.

With a whimper in the back of her throat, she arched her back, rubbing her nipples against my chest. *Oh fuck, yes.* My hips gave an involuntary jerk and I knew I was going to come if I didn't stop.

Despite the overwhelming desire, guilt started its insidious creep through me. She didn't deserve this. The first woman who could arouse me in years. And I was acting like a strung-out addict.

With a growl, I pushed away from her onto the far end of the couch. My lungs burned, desperate for oxygen. My skin itched, desperate to touch her again. Everything slowed to a stop, and my brain cataloged every single thing about the moment.

Her legs were slightly parted with her shorts riding up, exposing acres of skin. Her shirt had ridden up past her bottom rib, and I swallowed hard. Another inch and I'd be able to see the underside of her breast. Three more inches and I'd have nipple.

My cock twitched. Jesus, I wanted to taste her so bad. *No. Stop it. You can't have her.* "Fuck. Bollocks. Shit."

Blinking, she sat up. "I—what was that?"

I ran my hands through my hair. "I'm a wanker. I had

this dream, and you were standing there and..." I let my voice trail. "It won't happen again."

Who the hell was I kidding? If she was going to move in with me for a couple of weeks, it was bound to happen again unless I got my shit together.

She swallowed hard and pushed herself to standing. She didn't say a word as she stalked into the bathroom and closed the door.

I was never out of control. Why couldn't I sort myself out with her? The proposal last night had been playing the part. But kissing her, bollocks, that had been the best moment of the night... and the stupidest. She'd tasted so good, so sweet. For days I'd been able to convince myself that I'd imagined how good she tasted that first night. But now I knew I hadn't made it up.

I stared at the door for several minutes then cursed. I'd almost jeopardized everything, all because I couldn't keep my hands off of her. *Get it together, Xan.* I needed her. I couldn't fuck this up.

❧

Xander

I may have just pulled this madness off. I surveyed the guests as we milled about the balcony for breakfast. I'd spent the majority of the previous day in meetings with various board members where they'd asked about why I wanted to be on the board. My commitment. Why the work was so important to me, given my career. I'd been as honest as I could be, giving just enough of the truth to be believable. I could hardly tell them I only wanted to expose Alistair.

While I was busy with meetings, Imani had been lumped with the other plus ones. Charlotte had taken a particular liking to her. Which could be bad or good, depending on how I looked at it. Truth was, I should have been more worried, but that money was as important to her as getting on the board was to me. So I had to hope she gave a good show. By the time I returned to the room at the end of the evening, she was fast asleep.

It wasn't exactly like I was avoiding her. I was just avoiding being in an enclosed room with her, which was entirely different. After what had happened when she woke me from my dream, I figured it was best to give her a wide berth for a bit.

We'd do friendly things. I'd show her around Paris. Stay at my flat. It was spacious with two bedrooms. Plenty of room. At the very least I wouldn't have to hear her soft breathing and wonder about how peaceful she looked in sleep. Or think about how soft her skin was. Or worse, want to touch it again.

I hated the way she made me lose control. Every time I was around her, I felt like I was spiraling down, about to crash.

Then of course I'd kissed her last night and made matters worse. And just like the other night, I'd been ready to have her on the spot. It was as though her lips were my own personal brand of dynamite. I went to sleep still half hard from that kiss. I wasn't sure what had triggered my nightmare. I was no shrink, but I was pretty sure emotional and physical upheaval didn't help keep nightmares at bay. I'd need to figure something out very quickly. Otherwise, living together was going to be a big fucking problem, even in a place as big as mine.

My morning meeting with LeClerc and the rest of the board couldn't have gone better. The women on the board had been easier to convince than the men. My work spoke for itself. But the tricky part was using the right combination of charm without overdoing it. If I used too much, they'd assume everything Alistair said was truth. If I used too little, they could assume I didn't care enough about the job. If I were going to be the man behind the brand of the trust, I'd need to give a shit and have my mind focused on the right things.

Imani glanced up in surprise when she saw me at the bottom of the stairs. "Oh, Xander. I didn't expect to see you." Her tongue darted out and moistened her lower lip. "I know we leave in the morning, so I'm taking the chance to see the city. I'll be back tonight."

I shook my head. "*We* are headed into the city. We'll stay at my place tonight."

"Uh," she sputtered. "You don't have to do that. I know you're busy."

"Free as a bird. I finished up my final meeting this morning. I made you a promise, and I intend to keep it. Unless there's a reason you don't want to go to Paris with me?"

She pressed her lips together firmly. "Nope, nothing at all. Ready when you are."

"Great."

I'd opted for a car and driver into the city. Driving in Paris required a certain level of insanity and rage, and I wasn't in the mood today. "What would you like to do first?"

Her eyes darkened, and her gaze dipped to my lips. If she kept looking at me like that, I was just going to give her what she wanted.

She shook her head and cleared her throat. "Well, how about the Eiffel Tower?"

"Do you mind if we do that one tonight when it's all lit up? My flat is right near there. How about *Sacré-Coeur*? We'll need to be a little strategic since we only have today."

"Sure. I'm not fussy. I just want to see it. Lead the way."

"I figured we could celebrate tonight with dinner?"

"Celebrate. Right. I take it they gave you the job?"

"Not yet. They'll need to take a vote back in London.

But thanks to you and whatever you said to Charlotte, it's looking up. So as soon as we get back, I'll wire you."

"Yeah, just how is that going to work when we get back, exactly? Because Vincent Price back there thinks we live together."

The snort of laughter came out of nowhere. Damn, this woman could make me laugh. "You're right. He does sort of resemble Price. I dunno. You come stay at my place for a couple of weeks. After the next board vote, we'll have a quiet little breakup. No big deal."

"That's what you said about coming to Paris."

Damn, why couldn't I ever get my words right around her? I'd talked countless women out of their La Perla. Why couldn't I have a simple conversation? "I guess I did. I'm willing to concede it's a tad more complicated than I might have suggested."

"Just a tad?" Her laugh was incredulous.

My grin came easy. "A smidge, really."

"Can I ask you something?"

I swallowed hard, pretty sure I wasn't going to like answering her. "Of course. I'll tell you the truth if I can." The hell I would. The last thing I needed was her any closer to me than she already was.

"Yesterday, what was the nightmare about? When you kissed me, it was like you were trying to run from something. It seemed almost like you were afraid to touch me."

I'm terrified you'll find out my secret. Because I know if

I touch you the way I want, you'll abandon me eventually. But I couldn't say any of those things to her, so I settled on, "Because it's better in the long run for you if I don't touch you."

"But you want to?"

I swallowed, trying desperately to cool off my parched throat. "I think you already know the answer to that." I was saved from having to delve too deep into that subject by our arrival into the city.

CHAPTER FOURTEEN

XANDER

After a full day in Paris, I led Imani into my flat around seven. I'd called ahead to my housekeeper to make sure it was clean and dusted and stocked with some food for the night and for breakfast. I'd also had her open all the windows and shutters.

Imani gasped the moment she stepped into the flat behind me. She'd insisted on carrying some of the bags, but she dropped them in the doorway as she half jogged, half stumbled to the window. "Are you fucking kidding me right now? I've completely forgotten about my aching feet because of this view."

I grinned. The view alone was the sole reason I'd bought the place. It had cost me a fortune, but it was completely worth it. I couldn't describe how I felt every time I walked into the flat. We were close enough to the

Eiffel Tower to have the lights brightly illuminate my living area. I'd kept some of the Parisian charm of the place, like the original wood floor, and I'd rehabbed the chandeliers, but everything else I'd upgraded with modern fixtures.

Imani didn't move from the window, so I picked up her bags and carted them with mine into the living room. I might have gone a little overboard with the shopping today. I'd bought her a couple of things to help her look the part. All against her protests, of course. But the few things had quickly become many things. Not that we'd really be hitting up the town that often, but we needed to look the part of a young couple in love, so we'd need to go out. *Yeah, keep telling yourself that.*

I shook my head to clear the thought. We'd made a slight deviation from the plan, and I'd yet to course correct. I'd be able to properly manage that once we got back to London. "So it's safe to say the slack-jawed expression is because you like the view."

She danced giddily in place. "Remind me again why we haven't been staying here since we arrived? I mean this is insane."

I shrugged. "I used to spend more time here when I was doing fashion shoots. But once I got a more permanent gig at uni, it made sense to be in London more often. I don't know. I feel more relaxed here. In London I'm usually playing a part. But in Paris, I can just be who I am and not worry about disappointing anybody. This is one of my favorite cities in the world."

She chewed her lip as she nodded slowly. "What comes in as a close second?"

I chewed my lip as I thought it over. "I think New York and Tokyo are in a heated battle for second."

"I'm surprised you didn't say London. This is beautiful, but I have a love affair with the queen's city."

I laughed. "Give Paris a proper chance. I thought for sure with this view it would be your favorite."

"God, it's so close. But I dunno. There's just something about London. Maybe because it represents escape for me. And today was such a breakneck pace. My feet might never recover."

"You'll be back. Hell, if things go well, I'll bring you back myself. And I didn't take you to the Eiffel Tower earlier because I wanted you to see it like this first, at night. For most Parisians, it's a bit of an eyesore, but I personally love it. I'll take you up first thing in the morning if you want, before we head back to the chateau."

"Yes, I want. If I'd done nothing else today, this would have been enough."

"You're easy to please."

"Pretty much." She laughed. "Give me bright and shiny any day. It's part of why I started performing on stage. I loved the dance costumes when I was little. I didn't start acting until I was almost in high school. I was all about the sequins and the glitter."

I slid a glance to the simple band I'd given her. I would have to replace it with something better when we got back. As part of the charade, of course. "When is your show?" I asked, changing the subject, desperate to get on level ground again.

"Late May, so six weeks or so. We'll do a special performance at the Old Vic too. There will be casting agents there and representation, so it's a good chance to get seen."

"Sounds like a really big deal."

She nodded, still staring out the window. "It is. I'm scared shitless."

"I've seen you in character. You were bloody amazing."

Imani ducked her head. "Thank you. I hope I don't disappoint Charles. I know some people didn't want me in the lead."

"Wankers, the lot of them. No one who sees you on stage will think you don't belong there."

She ducked her head. "Thank you. That's probably the sweetest thing anyone has ever said to me."

"Sweet. That's what everyone calls me." I cocked my head. "Let me show you around the flat. You can have this room. It's got the best view of the Eiffel Tower."

"Where are you sleeping?"

"I'm across the flat. If you need anything, just give me a shout."

"You must be so relieved to get back in your own bed again instead of the couch."

I doubted it would help me sleep any better knowing she was just down the hall, but I was willing to try anything. "Something like that." Leaving her to get settled, I took a long, hot shower, letting the grime of the Paris crowds wash off of me. Afterward, I donned a pair of pajama bottoms. I normally slept naked, but that was a hell of a lot of temptation. And if she did come in needing anything, she probably didn't want a bird's eye view of my God-given assets.

Now all I had to do was pray for a dreamless sleep. But the moment I heard crying, I knew sleep wasn't in the cards for me.

⋆ ⋆

Imani

This was the Paris I'd dreamed of. After washing my hair, I'd sat in front of the window, twisting it in chunky sections and staring up. If I believed in fairy tales, today was that perfect kind of fairy-tale day.

My phone rang, and I dragged it out of my purse, recognizing the home phone number on display. "Ebony?"

There was a pause. "No, it's your father, you know, that man you don't bother to call anymore." His words slurred together, and I knew right away he'd been drinking.

Nevertheless, guilt slithered its way down my spine. He was right. I hadn't called. I'd been making it a point to avoid him. Because more often than not, he had been drinking, and our conversations usually ended in a fight about money, abandoning the family to go to London, leaving him with the burden of raising Ebony. He seemed to forget that Ebony was his child, not mine. "Dad, how are you? Is Ebony okay?"

"Of course she's okay. I take care of her, don't I?"

No. Actually, he didn't. I did most of the work, paid all the bills electronically, had organized for groceries to be delivered. But that didn't matter because I loved my sister and I would do anything for her, including be the parent. "What's going on, Dad?"

"I want you to stop filling your sister's head with that nonsense about her moving to London. There is no scenario where I let her just move."

"What? You don't want her to have a future? You won't be able to stop her if she wants to come." But before I could bring Ebony to London, I had his mortgage bill to pay. But I wasn't bringing that up. I was too tired for that epic kind of rumble.

"Well, I'm not going to pay for it. I already told her. And she can forget about her prom." His words slurred again, and I pinched the bridge of my nose. He'd never forgiven me for wanting out of that depressing house after my mother's death. He thought I should have stayed home and gone to State University of New York. When my mother had died my sophomore year of high school, he'd completely unraveled and started drinking more heavily.

It had started slow, with him forgetting to pick us up from school, then the power getting shut off. He couldn't manage the day-to-day caretaking of Ebony, so I had done it. He owned his own business, so his employees had taken over the lion's share of the effort. But when he'd missed a payroll, I'd been the one to step in and set up automatic payments. And when I'd told him I'd be leaving for school, he'd crumbled. But I knew I couldn't have stayed in that house any longer without killing off a piece of myself. So I'd chosen to save myself rather than stay for my sister.

When my father was sober, things were good. I could see pieces of the man I loved. But those days were rare. The guilt I felt for leaving my sister behind overwhelmed me some days. But I was trying to fix that now. "I'm working to take that burden off of you. It doesn't have to be hard, Daddy. It'll make her happy."

"You never wanted to help me. You ran away as soon as you could."

Because he'd suffocated me. Because I should have been worried about school, but because he couldn't deal, I shouldered the burden. And it was a heavy one. "I followed my dream. I'm sorry that hurt you. But it's too much. You're hurting Ebony."

"You don't know what you're talking about. You think

I'm doing this to spite you? I'm not. Business isn't good, Imani. I have to lay people off. Those extras, I actually can't afford them. And there you are living a highflying lifestyle instead of being here contributing. All you're doing is filling Ebony's head with dreams I'll never be able to fulfill."

I blinked away the stinging in my eyes as I looked up at the Eiffel Tower. This was highflying. It was a dream, and I'd see it through for my sister. "What do you want from me, Dad? I'll do it. I don't want to fight with you anymore. I'm doing the best I can."

"You want to help? Instead of filling your sister's mind with dreams she can't have, focus on the things she needs now."

Why hadn't Ebony mentioned her prom? Probably because she was more worried about the mortgage. "How much is it for prom, Dad? I can help."

"Dress, limo, tickets, you do the math."

The walls closed in just a little tighter, and I fought to breathe. Why did this have to be so damn hard? "I'll talk to Ebony and take care of it."

He was silent for so long I thought he'd either passed out or hung up. "Why did you have to leave?"

"Daddy, I—" But he was gone. The dial tone sounded in my ear. *Crying will not solve anything. Crying will not solve anything.* It didn't matter what I told myself, hot tears splashed my cheeks as I stared up at the Eiffel Tower.

Xander

What the hell was I doing? I had zero experience with women and tears. When I did, usually *I* was the cause and wanted to avoid being kicked in the nuts.

But as far as I could tell, I wasn't the cause of these tears. But just like the day at RADA, the pull to take care of her was stronger than my pull to run. There was no way I could ignore the tears. Especially not in this flat. It was Paris, so it was considerably smaller than my place in London, and the walls were paper thin.

I knocked, but it took several moments for her to tell me to come in.

When I entered, her eyes were rimmed red, and despite her attempts at wiping the moisture off her cheeks, tears still clung stubbornly to her lashes. She was on her bed, and her hair was damp and extremely curly. She'd tucked it into a high bun at the top of her head. She wore pajama bottoms and one of the silky camis I'd bought her.

Oh hell. I could see the perfect outline of her nipples. *Eyes on the prize, you lecherous ass.* I dragged my gaze up and pinned it to her red-rimmed eyes. "What's the matter?"

She shook her head and swiped at the tears with the back of her hand. "I'm sorry." She shook her head. "I didn't mean to bug you."

"You're not. Clearly you're upset." I rubbed a hand

over the back of my neck. I had no idea what to do or say. Comforting someone was not in my wheelhouse.

"It's my headache."

"Not just *your* headache; I want to know." The words were right, but I sounded annoyed. I needed to try for nurturing and less angry.

With a sigh, she said, "I got a call from home."

Did I hold her? Did she want to be left alone? "I don't understand."

She rubbed at her nose with the back of her hand. "My father has a way of laying on the guilt. Usually, I can brush it off and ignore him. But I don't know. Today it just hurt more."

"Do you want to talk about it?"

"Thank you. But you don't have to do this. I'm okay. It's not your problem."

I tried to lighten the mood a little and maybe make her smile. I couldn't take tears. Especially not *her* tears. "I can be a good friend. Don't let the bad-boy smirk and devilish good looks fool you. Let me help."

She looked up at the ceiling and sighed. "My father is what you would call a functional alcoholic. Except, these days, not so functional."

"Why, what's changed?"

"Ever since my mom died when I was fifteen, he's been deteriorating."

My first thought was I was not equipped for this

conversation. But for once it didn't stop me from wanting to help fix it. "Shit, I'm sorry. At least you're here and you don't have to deal with that on a day-to-day basis.

Her shoulders shook slightly. "That's the crappy thing. I left my sister behind. I got a full ride to RADA, and I bounced. At least that's how it feels. The plan has always been to bring Ebony with me as soon as she was done with school, but Dad's getting worse. I don't want to leave her there."

"Is there someone else she can stay with? A friend? Family?"

"No family except me. And I'm pretty sure her friends would take her in for her senior year, but she's been accepted at a school here. It just costs more than our father's willing to pay." Imani shook her head. "I told you. It's a long, screwed-up story."

I ran my hand through my hair. "Money—is that why you were at the Notting Hill flat?"

"Yeah. He neglected to pay the mortgage for a while. Ebony called me freaking out, so I thought I could at least put out that fire."

Damn. "That's a lot of guilt you're carrying around. You might want to take it easy on yourself."

She shook her head. "You don't get it."

I shrugged. "Maybe I do. More than you know."

I approached the bed cautiously. When was the last time I'd comforted someone? In particular a woman?

Seduction, I knew how to do. Nurturing, not so much. I could figure this out. How hard could it be? I sat and reached for her, wrapping an arm around her. She slumped into me.

"I'm sorry. I'm not usually so emotional."

I smoothed her hair. I'd seen it done enough to fake it. "It's okay. Of course this is going to affect you." I was getting the hang of this. Easy. All I had to do was keep my eyes... I didn't mean to let my gaze stray from hers, but it dipped for just a second to the pebbled peaks of her nipples under her cami, and blood rushed to my cock.

Bollocks. Time to go. Releasing her, I stood up abruptly, careful to keep my growing erection under wraps. "Listen, I was going to make some cocoa. Would you like some?"

In the muted light, with her blinking her dark eyes up at me, I locked my jaw against the rush of need. She didn't need my particular brand of fucked up. She was plenty screwed up on her own. My cock and I had a silent exchange on the matter.

Xander: Shut up and go back to sleep, you wanker.

Cock: Bollocks, like I was asleep, given she's around.

Xander: You're a cunt. We're leaving her alone.

Cock: Fucker. Or even better, fuck *her*.

And so it went in my head, back and forth, until she reached up and took my hand. "Xander." Her teeth grazed her bottom lip and my resolve wavered. But it was the whispered way she said, "Please stay," that made me realize I was going to lose the battle.

"Imani..." Fuck, why did my voice sound so husky? I cleared my throat. "I—"

"Please stay. Talk to me about whatever. I know, I'm probably crossing a million lines or something. But, I dunno—"

Fuck. My cock twitched, but I refused to concede defeat. I could do something unselfish. I scrubbed a hand over my face. "Scoot over." She slid over in the bed and I lay next to her, *on top* of the sheets. "If you snore, I'm out of here."

Her bottom lip quivered, but she met my gaze levelly. "Thank you."

As I lay there talking to her, I tried to remember the last time I'd done something completely unselfish.

That's easy...never.

CHAPTER FIFTEEN

IMANI

orture. If I had to describe the prospect of living with the sexiest man I'd ever seen in my life, I'd classify it as torture. Not like I didn't have enough on my plate. Like my sister. Like the finances for my family. Thankfully, thanks to this weekend, I'd managed to make that first mortgage payment to put the bank off for a minute.

But I had other problems on the horizon. Like having to work with the devil incarnate. I still had several days until the official start of rehearsals. I had to figure out how I was going to deal with Ryan. *You are not a victim.* And certainly not *his* victim.

Screw what Ryan wanted. I had to talk to Charles. *He won't believe you.* I had to do something. Because rehearsals would be going for weeks, and there was no way

I'd survive having to stare into his eyes every day. Even I wasn't that strong.

When the car pulled up to the glass-and-chrome building on the South Bank, I peered up at London's perpetually gray sky. If I craned my head to the left, I could see the London Eye and Westminster. Restaurants and pubs dotted the street, as did boutiques and several corner shops. Behind the sleek, modern building I could clearly see the Thames River with the barges and house-boats floating along. I knew the area well. Just down the way a little bit was the National Theater.

Xander tapped my knee, then immediately yanked his hand back as if he'd been burned. With a tight smile, he cocked his head. "C'mon, let's go in. We can get you settled, then I'll send someone to your flat to get anything you need." He slid out of the car and held out a hand to me but then obviously thought better of it and just stepped aside, giving me room.

As I slid out, I glanced up again. "Where are we?"

"My flat." He said it slowly like he was talking to a child or an imbecile. "Remember? You agreed to this."

Funny, jackass. "This isn't Notting Hill."

"Oh," he muttered and glanced down at his shoes. "I don't live there..." His voice trailed off.

It only took a moment for reality to dawn. "Right." Apparently, that was just his fuck pad. *Fantastic.* What did I even know about this guy besides his name?

Once in the elevator, he touched my elbow gently. "Having second thoughts?"

Yes. *No.* I needed the money, and living with him for a couple of weeks wouldn't kill me. Sex wasn't part of the bargain, so I could do this. "It's not that. I'm just realizing I don't know anything about you besides your name." I frowned, "Or is that a fake placeholder one too?"

He smirked, and I forgot to breathe for two beats. "It's Alexander Andrew Chase."

I stuck out my hand. "Nice to meet you. I'm Imani Leah Aysem Brooks."

He considered for a moment. "Leah, I like it."

"Looks like we're doing everything a little backward."

His grin flashed and my belly flipped. God, that should be outlawed. He looked so boyish and teasing when he smiled like that. Granted, I also liked the intense version of him very much. I admonished myself as heat pooled between my thighs. That was so not happening.

"Imani?"

I blinked up at him in surprise. "Yeah?"

"Did you hear me?"

Damn it, had he been talking while I ogled him? "Sorry. Just daydreaming. What did you say?"

He looked me up and down. His voice dropped low when he spoke. "Just what were you thinking about, exactly?"

"Oh my God, would you stop with the patented Xander Chase seduction voice? It's distracting."

He laughed. "I should have my seduction patented? Wicked. Unlike my brother, I don't have patents. I've always wanted one of my own. So, you want to explain just how distracting I am?"

"And swell up your enormous head even more? No. I do not." I laughed.

He cocked his head and winked at me. "Which head would you be talking about?"

I covered my eyes. "You're impossible."

His laugh made me want to melt into a pile of goo, but I steeled myself against it. If I were going to make it for the next few weeks with him, I'd have to get used to it.

The elevator let us out on the penthouse level, and my breath caught. For starters, the place was huge. So much room I could probably even lose him in there. Everything was hypermodern, from the low chairs and chrome fixtures to the white, gray and black palette for all the furniture. But he'd added warmth with the pictures on the walls and the accessories.

The pillows and throw rugs contained an eclectic mix of African, Middle Eastern, and Asian influences. The photos were simply exquisite. Like the accessories, the walls were an eclectic mix of photos from all around the world. "My God, Xander. This is amazing." They were mostly stunning landscapes, but quite a few candid portraits as well. He also peppered in some abstract work.

A light flush stained his cheeks. "Uh, glad you like it. Just bits and bobs from the places I've been. And my favorite photographs."

"It's perfect." I could probably spend days just studying the photos on the walls.

He cleared his throat. "There are two master bedrooms down here and two smaller bedrooms upstairs. I'll put you in one of the masters if that's okay. There's more than enough room. No need for us to be on top of each other."

My lips twitched, and I couldn't help myself. "That's what she said."

Xander blinked at me once, then again. Then the sound of his laugh ricocheted off the walls of the flat. "Oh my God, I am engaged to a twelve-year-old boy."

I looked down at my body. "With tits."

His gaze flickered to my chest, then back to my face again. "You are probably going to be the death of me."

"Probably." I shrugged. "So, what are my chances that you've got a bus schedule around here somewhere? Or can you tell me which way is the nearest tube station? I've got to start with some logistics of getting around to rehearsals now that I'll be staying here."

"Don't worry about it. We'll have a car service take you."

"You're kidding, right? I take the bus all the time. The

tube too. It's perfectly safe. If it's going to be past midnight, I'll call a mini cab or something."

He frowned, then folded his arms over his chest. I'd seen that look before. He had no intention on budging. It was the look he'd given me at rehearsal that day. "You'll take a car. It's safer and more convenient for you."

"I appreciate it. I do. But honestly, I need to figure out how I'm going to do things on my own."

"You forget you're playing the part of my fiancée, right? And it looks bad if I've got you hopping on the bus."

"Oh, come on. That's just some elitist bullshit."

He stepped into my space, crowding me. "You realize that the paparazzi can follow you onto a train, and there'll be no getting away from them. Same with a bus."

"Oh, come on, you said it yourself. There should be minimal paparazzi."

"Why are you being so stubborn about this? Why can't you just do what I ask?"

I jutted my chin out. "Because I don't like to be told what to do. This is my independence you're talking about. I need freedom to move about. Go out with the cast, that sort of thing."

The frown lines on his forehead deepened. "You mean go out with Ryan?"

I would rather be flayed alive, but I wasn't giving him any more reason to throw his weight around. "Who I go out with is none of your business."

"It is for the next couple of weeks."

We were nearly chest to chest now, both of our breathing choppy and uneven. His gaze dipped to my lips. And I licked them in an automatic subconscious response. Xander's pupils dilated, and for a long moment he stilled on the precipice of giving me a kiss.

But then he lifted his head and took a very deliberate step backward. His gaze shifted to my eyes and he swallowed. "Please. I'm asking nicely."

His clear, gray gaze implored me. "Fine. If it will get you off my case." If this battle of wills was any indication, then it was going to be a long two weeks.

Imani

I tapped my foot impatiently outside of the rehearsal hall. I'd been trying to reach Charles for two days since I got back, but he hadn't had any time to meet until an hour before I was supposed to go on and rehearse with Ryan.

"Imani, I'm so sorry I couldn't meet until now. As you can imagine, there is a lot of press surrounding the show, so I've been working with marketing and PR. How is my star doing?"

"Hi, Charles. Is there any way we can go in to chat for a minute?"

"Sure." He led me in and turned on the lights illuminating the stage. There was something about seeing the spotlight on the stage that always relaxed me. It was the one place I felt at home. Like I could explore every single thing I was feeling in a safe way. In real life, I had generally learned to block out the less pleasant emotions by working hard and burying them deep.

Once we were seated in one of the center rows, he asked, "What's going on with you, Imani? Normally you don't let an upcoming show stress you out."

"Who says I'm stressed?"

He raised a brow. "Besides being your advisor, I saw your audition tape. I hand-selected you to be in the program. I fought for you to stay. I know *you*."

I sighed. Not as well as he thought he did. "Okay, I'm sorry to have to come to you with this, but—" I paused, trying to find the best words to use. "Ryan and I, we—"

His smile was fatherly and endearing when he interrupted me. "You used to go out? Imani, I know that already. You two were very discreet at the time, and I figured it was none of my business if it didn't interfere with your studies or your performance. And to be honest, he told me about it when I cast him. He didn't want there to be any tension between you two."

Ryan had preempted me? What had the sack of lying, festering shit said? "I didn't know he'd already spoken to you."

"Yes, he explained that your relationship was... volatile,

but that you had mostly worked through your issues and you'd be able to work together."

No, we would not be able to work together. I ground my teeth as I willed my body to still. Volatile? Is that what he called it? What he'd done to me? As if we were just a passionate couple who fought?

"Charles, I assure you that I'm a professional and I can do my job. And I don't know what he told you exactly, but I have real concerns about working with him."

My mentor's brows drew down. "I don't understand."

"I—" I held my breath. What I said today would determine my future. Would he believe me? Maybe if I'd been the first to speak to Charles then he would be more likely to. But since Ryan had spoken to him first, it would look like sour grapes. Or worse, like I was being a diva.

Charles could determine the trajectory of my career. A career Ryan had already started to establish. But I was smart enough to know I couldn't be alone with the asshole. Thinking fast I said, "I just mean that given our past, to keep the rumors quiet, maybe we shouldn't rehearse alone. My concern is for the integrity of the show." My throat burned with the need to say the words out loud. *He raped me. He held me down when I said no and forced me to have sex with him, and then he told me there was nothing I could do about it because I was his girlfriend and no one would believe me.*

But I couldn't spit out those words. Instead I spoke

about the show and what it meant to me. I was a liar. But I was not going to be anyone's victim. Especially not Ryan's. Charles studied me, but then nodded. "I can see where you're going. A play like this, the media would be all over it if they thought you were in a romantic relationship in real life." He seemed to consider the idea. "I mean it wouldn't really hurt if you were. It might even boost interest."

"No." Something vile and insidious wrapped around my spine. I would not do that. "Not going to happen, Charles. It's about the play." Then I threw out the one thing I had in my pocket. "Besides, I'm with Xander Chase."

His brows popped up. "I was under the impression you'd only met that day of the shoot."

"We were trying to keep things quiet." Technically true. "It's been sort of a whirlwind. So you see, there's no chance of cozy publicity shots with Ryan. But I want to maintain the integrity of the show, regardless."

"It's an odd request, but if I can accommodate Ryan's private dressing room, I can do this for you. We'll have a PA on hand who can even live tweet rehearsals or whatever. Keep the social media interest up."

I breathed a small sigh of relief, even though it wasn't exactly what I'd been looking for. I should have anticipated that Ryan would try to hamstring me from ever telling anybody, but I knew what he'd done to me. I might have to work with him for the sake of my future, but I was walking in with my eyes wide open, knowing the devil I was working with. There would be no cozy rehearsals with just the two of us. And I was packing pepper spray for sure. It didn't matter what I had to do, I was never going to be that naive girl again, the one who trusted so blindly. Nor was I going to roll over and play dead.

This was my show, my chance to shine. I was not going to be afraid. Not of that asshole. I was stronger than he was. I had to be.

"Thank you, Charles. I appreciate it."

The door to the hall opened, and I could see the figure backlit in the doorway. My stomach rolled and I swallowed hard. *Breathe, Imani. You can do anything. You can survive anything.* It was time to go to work.

CHAPTER SIXTEEN

XANDER

I hitched my camera bag over my shoulder. "I'm telling you she's deliberately trying to drive me crazy." Even though the two of us had settled into a routine over the last four days, it was hardly comfortable. I certainly wasn't getting much sleep. I'd called Lex for support, but somehow my brother was not backing me up.

"Xan, I doubt that. I mean, what's she doing?" Lex asked.

"For starters, she's employing some kind of female guerrilla warfare tactics because the whole place smells like her. Everywhere I go, it's coconut and hibiscus." It was so bad I was in a state of permanent erection with her around.

"Nefarious. She should be drawn and quartered." Lex was no help.

"I see you don't understand my pain. I'm telling you she's trying to drive me slowly mad and you make jokes. You're not there, you don't see the bras she leaves hanging on the drying rack in the washroom. The way she walks around half dressed in shorts so tiny she might as well only be wearing panties." The bras were the worst, because every time I went in there to wash my workout gear, all I could think about were her C-cups.

One more thing I'd learned about her was that she hated for anyone to do anything for her. She insisted on washing her own laundry instead of letting the laundry service handle it. When I left dishes in the sink, knowing that housekeeping would handle it, she went ahead and washed them. When I complained, she rolled her eyes and told me it was a simple thing to do on her own. She didn't need help for that. Even something so simple as grocery bags. She insisted on carrying her fair share.

Lex's booming laugh rang clear on the phone. "Have you tried asking her to wear more clothing when she's walking around?"

Why would I do that? "What, are you insane? I'm not a fool. I'm just saying she's doing it deliberately. But I can certainly enjoy the view."

"Here's a thought. You could try scratching the itch. You'll certainly be more relaxed that way."

Hell yes. "With her? Not going to happen. I need to stay focused."

Lex merely laughed. "If you say so. Speaking of focus, any word from LeClerc?"

"Not yet, but I should hear something soon."

"Okay, I've made the final stock purchases, so I'm just waiting on your signal."

"Cheers to that." I leaned against the elevator door as I rode to the penthouse. I wondered if she'd be home already, sitting around in her shorts again showing off her lean legs and perfect behind. Rehearsals hadn't officially started, but she'd gone in several times for wardrobe measurements. And each time she'd taken the car without too much complaint.

"Either way, this will all be over soon. And then maybe you can focus on you for a change," Lex reminded me.

"Yeah, focus on me. Whatever that means." The elevator bell dinged on the top floor, and the doors slid open. The lights in the living room and kitchen were on, but there was no sign of her. "Oh, honey, I'm home." I snickered as I dropped my camera bag on the coffee table next to her script. I might complain to Lex, but I kind of liked the noise she brought to my environment. She was tidy, but she did have the tendency to spread. A script here, a book there. The laundry detergent in the wash-room. Her scent... everywhere.

"Lex, I'm hopping off."

"Yeah, you do that. And do try to play nice with your houseguest."

Easier said than done.

Imani

There was no way I would get used to sleeping in the total silence of Xander's flat. His sound-proofed windows completely canceled any street noise, and it was too eerie. I also didn't want to waste electricity by sleeping with the television on. It wasn't my place, so I was trying to be a good guest. Unfortunately, it meant I couldn't sleep.

Standing on tiptoe, I opened the cupboard looking for the hot cocoa. Was it this one? Maybe the one over the stove. I should have paid closer attention when he was showing me around. And I certainly wasn't going to go and wake him up to ask.

When I finally found the damn cocoa, it was on the topmost shelf. "Fantastic."

I groaned as I tried to inch it off the shelf with the tips of my fingers.

"Here, let me get that."

Xander's low voice directly behind me startled me, and I jumped back into his chest, sending the cocoa tipping over—spilling it over the both of us and the counter.

"Shit. Sorry." Exasperated, I shook my head. "I'm so sorry. I was totally trying not to wake you, and now I've made a fucking mess."

He dusted cocoa out of his hair. "Relax. It's okay."

"I was really trying not to wake you up. I swear."

"It's fine, Imani. Believe me, I wasn't asleep." He gestured upward. "It was my fault. I shouldn't have startled you."

Except it wasn't fine. I was wide awake. And he was standing right in front of me, practically pressing that gorgeous, shirtless body into me. Without thinking, I reached out and dusted some of the cocoa off his pecs. It should be criminal for the man to ever put on a shirt. It took me several seconds to realize I was brushing my fingertips over his flesh and that he hadn't moved a muscle.

Stop touching him. Stop. Fingers off. Hands down. My brain gave the command, but it was like the signal was blocked.

He licked his bottom lip, and my world went into slow motion. Underneath my fingertips, I could feel his heartbeat thudding in time with mine. I didn't think anything could match the thundering heartbeat in my chest.

"Imani." He whispered my name and toyed with a coil of my hair. "You have cocoa in your hair."

In that breath of silence, I knew he was going to kiss me. And I had no idea how I felt about it. I *wanted* his body pressed into mine. Wanted that wild need that he sparked in me every time he was around me. Wanted to feel that free-fall he'd sparked that first night again.

But it didn't matter how I felt in the moment. If I went

there with him, I'd be changed forever. I'd had sex since that awful night two years ago. Decent sex. Nothing earth-shattering, but nice all the same. Even managed to have a couple of orgasms. But mostly, I just wondered what all the fuss was about.

After what had happened with Ryan, I'd gone to talk to someone. It was the one right thing I'd done. The one thing I'd clung to in the complete chaos that followed. It had helped. Enough so that I recognized that sleeping with Xander would be different.

I was self-aware enough to know if I actually slept with Xander it would break something inside of me. I wouldn't recover. Something inside me would bond to him, and 'decent sex' would never do for me again.

I cleared my throat. "I'm just going to go back to bed."

"I should let you."

He should. But he didn't move out of the way. And my body didn't want that. The heat pooling between my thighs and the throbbing need inside me rooted me to the spot. I wanted him to kiss me. I wanted his hands on my body. I wanted him to make love to me. Wanted him to make me come, to teach me how to break free. I craved that elusive feeling only he could pull from me, and I wanted to experience that again. Even if it wasn't real. Even if it didn't last.

"Imani, you're not going."

"You haven't let me out." I didn't want to be let out.

He shook his head. "I don't think I can." He sucked in a deep breath then cupped my cheek. "I'm going to break my promise."

Yes, please. "Okay," I whispered.

Xander

I inhaled deeply before pressing my lips to hers. When I teased my tongue between her lips, she sighed as I licked into her mouth, stroking deep, turning up the temperature. I was so fucked.

She was very quickly becoming an addiction. With every taste I was falling further and further into the abyss. I'd heard her rustling out here, trying to be quiet, and I knew she couldn't sleep either.

Taking over the kiss, I angled her head so I could slide my tongue in deeper, tasting her more fully. Her lips were so soft. So perfect. I could kiss her for hours and never get bored. When she made this happy purring sound in the back of her throat, my blood hummed.

As I kissed her, I pressed my body into hers, needing to be in contact with as much of her as possible. I wanted to bury my cock deep inside her tight walls. For over a week, every night, all I'd dreamed about was pulling orgasm after orgasm out of her.

Muffling a curse, I lifted her and sat her on the countertop, stepping between her legs. A charge of electricity ran through me the moment my pajama-clad cock came into contact with her sweet center. All that separated us was the cotton of her shorts and my pajama bottoms.

She lifted her hips, bringing her core closer to me and I groaned, not daring to stop. This was what I wanted. This was what I needed. I *needed* her. And it scared the shit out of me. But I didn't dare stop. Couldn't stop.

When Imani rolled her hips into mine, my hips jerked. She was so responsive. I snuck my hands under her tank top, and she sucked in a shuddering breath.

God, she was so bloody soft. Over the last week, it was easy to imagine that I'd fabricated how soft she was, but I hadn't.

My thumbs skimmed up her ribcage, and I could feel her holding her breath as I traversed each of her ribs. When I reached the underside of her breasts, a shudder rolled through her body.

I wanted her to need me as much as I needed her. Gently, I palmed her breasts. Her breathing shallowed, and she threw her head back. "Xander."

Jesus, fuck. Her breasts spilled out of my palms as I nuzzled her neck, seeking out my favorite spot, just behind her ear. Her thready pulse jumped under my lips and I wanted to make her feel like this forever. I inhaled deeply before tracing my thumbs over her nipples. Groaning low, Imani locked her legs around my waist and cried out.

The words slid off my tongue in a whisper. "Angel, you are so goddamned beautiful." Her scent completely intoxicated me, making me shake. "I can't get you out of my head."

When she dug her hands into my hair, I growled against her throat. The devil on my shoulder pushed me to take. *Take her. Have her. Forget her.* But I knew I wouldn't be forgetting this girl. Not if I touched her again.

Slowly, I drew back and struggled to get my breathing under control. "Go to bed, Imani." It hurt, but I let go of her and stepped back.

She blinked up at me, confused, dropping her hands. "I don't understand."

"I'm not the bloke you take out for kicks, Imani. I've been a bad boy." I scrubbed both hands down my face.

She hopped off the counter and readjusted her clothes. "For the record, I'm not looking for kicks. *You* kissed *me.* Stop dicking with me if you don't have the balls to do anything about it."

"I'm not dicking with you. You just don't know what you're dealing with."

"And God forbid you treat me like an adult and tell me instead of being so guarded." When she brushed past me, I didn't follow.

CHAPTER SEVENTEEN

XANDER

I was in the doghouse and I knew it. And I also knew Imani was right for putting me there. After that kiss, it was plain to me that I was cracking. We'd been back for just over a week, but I needed out of the house pronto. She would be home soon from rehearsal, and I couldn't spend another night cooped up with her in the house. If I did, there was no way I was stopping at just kissing. I would fuck her on every single flat surface of this place.

But worse than the complete nutter routine I played out with that kiss was the fact that I didn't know why I'd done it. *Yes, you do. You want to know if that night was a fluke. But you also like her.* Fluke or not, it didn't matter. It's not like I wanted to be with her. *Liar.* I wanted her, yes. She was the first woman I'd had an orgasm with in years.

Yes. But I didn't *want* to be with *anyone*. Let alone a girl who sang show tunes in the shower, who cleaned to de-stress, and who could recite every single line from *Sex and the City* ever written, verbatim.

I rubbed at my temple and tried to focus on the images on my laptop. I was supposed to be sorting the best candidates from the RADA shoot, but of course it meant doing nothing but thinking about Imani as she was staring at me with those haunting hazel eyes.

I slid my gaze to the clock. Seven p.m. She'd be home soon. *Git.* I was waiting for her like a nervous father. Sitting back, I rubbed at my eyes. I had problems, real problems that weren't going to go away, but instead of focusing on solutions, I was thinking of ways I could complicate my life. Too late for that.

One picture in particular caught my attention. It was a cast shot with Imani and Ryan at the forefront. Everyone was laughing and smiling, including Imani, but she was the only one where the humor didn't reach her eyes. Ryan had his arm wrapped around her. At first glance, it looked like all the others. But when I looked closer, I could tell she was pulling away from him. Like she actively wanted to be as far away from him as possible.

I'd been giving her shit about Ryan being her boyfriend, and she hadn't corrected me. Had I read what I'd seen in the courtyard the wrong way? I forced my mind to remember what exactly I'd seen that day. Ryan had his hands on her upper arms, and her head was tilted up toward him. I had assumed for a kiss. But maybe I'd been wrong about that. At the time, I'd been livid with irrational thoughts that Imani was Ryan's.

With some clarity of distance, I recalled the way she'd flinched when I'd said "boyfriend." I assumed she was worried about me saying something about Notting Hill. But with the number of times I'd mentioned Ryan since then, why hadn't she said more? Yeah, she'd said he wasn't her boyfriend, but she hadn't said anything about actively disliking him.

But my gut told me it was more than that. Something deeper. The first thought that ran through my head was to talk to her about it. *None of your business.* Yeah, she probably wouldn't appreciate that.

If I could just get away from Imani for a night. Stop obsessing about the way her tits fit in my hands or the way she sucked on my tongue. Or my favorite torturous, memory of how her wet cunt pulled at my fingers.

Jesus fucking Christ. I was going out. I'd go to the club with Lex and the boys. Work off a little steam. Everything would be fine. I just had to hang on a little longer... and not bend her over the armrest of the couch in the process.

Just as I picked up the phone to call my brother, Imani opened the door. Her eyes were red, and her face was devoid of makeup. It wasn't unusual for her to take the natural route on her face. The only reason I even noticed was because she'd been wearing makeup when she left. "All right?"

She nodded. "Yeah, just a tough rehearsal."

"You look like you've been crying."

She shrugged and plopped onto the couch. "That's because I have been. I talked to Ebony today too. Dad's in a mood. Then it was a tough set of scenes today that involved a lot of work with Ryan. So all in all, it was a shit day."

I tried to tread carefully. "I was actually going through your pictures today."

"Oh yeah? Anything usable? I'm usually horrid in photos. I feel awkward and usually make some insane face."

"I don't know about that, you looked great to me."

"That's because you're some kind of photography savant or something and managed to make me look good in a picture."

"Probably," I said with a smile and a smirk. But she barely cracked a smile, so I continued. "Look. I know I fucked up last night. You're right, I was a total prat, and I want to apologize." I deliberately didn't apologize for the kiss. I wasn't sorry at all.

Her brows shot up. "Really? I didn't think Xander Chase did apologies."

It might only have been a few days, but she knew me

well. I didn't normally do them. At least not before meeting her. "Yeah. Well, you deserve one."

Her mouth opened as if she wanted to say something, but then she shut it again. "Uh, thanks. That means a lot."

Nodding, I pressed forward. "Listen, I'm going on my gut here, but is there something going on with Ryan?"

She pushed to her feet. "I've told you a million times. No. He's not my fucking boyfriend, okay? I really wish you would stop jibing at me with that."

"Not like that." I sighed. Life was infinitely easier when I didn't give a fuck about someone else's feelings. "In one of the pictures, you just looked like you didn't want him touching you. Like you were really distressed by it." When her eyes misted over, I shifted in my seat. Was holding permissible?

"How about we say I'm not a fan and call it a day? The last thing I want is to spend any more of my brain power thinking about him."

Every instinct inside me said to push, but she looked bone weary, so I dropped it. And, to be honest, feelings just weren't my thing. "Okay, then. I know you're knackered, but maybe you feel like going out? I think maybe we've been a bit cooped up, on top of each other." That was an understatement. I was losing my bloody mind. *Why are you fighting it?* Maybe it wasn't the end of the world if I touched her.

"I don't know, Xander. I'm wrung out."

I cocked my head. I could leave her, but I didn't want her sitting here with those red eyes. I wanted to make her smile. If only for a little bit. "Come on. You've been working insane hours and researching and rehearsing. Just come out. Let off a little steam. I think we've both been a little tense."

She rolled her head to look at me. "Maybe you're right. If nothing else, I could certainly use a drink."

Imani

If this was how clubbing was done properly, then I had never been. That first night with Abbie and her friends was nothing compared to this. From the moment I'd walked in with Xander, everything had been VIP. No line, no cover, drinks appearing as if out of nowhere.

And Xander's friends? Completely unreal. I'd thought his brother, Lex, was gorgeous, But his friends were drool-worthy. Considering half of them were actual models it was no wonder, but still. One after another, he'd introduced them to me using the word *fiancée* as if it were a brand. "This is my fiancée, Imani." I was certainly some kind of fool, because those little words gave me a thrill.

He even had an in with the DJ. His friend Jasper was

Marc Ronson-worthy. He'd been the only one of the group who stared at me incredulously, then glared at Xander. "Fiancée? What's with you and Lex stealing all the beautiful girls?"

I recognized a flirt when I saw one. And he didn't help his cause when he took my hand and kissed it. And despite myself, out of everything going on that night, the part I enjoyed the most was Xander's attention. I was supposed to be tough like Teflon. But one smile from him and I was toast. Luckily this would only be for another couple of weeks. He'd assured me that once he was on the board we could stop and go back to our normal lives.

Abbie plopped onto the seat next to me. "Enjoying yourself?"

"Oh my God, yeah. This is crazy. This is so not my crowd, but it's really fun."

Abbie laughed. "Not my crowd either. It takes a little getting used to, honestly. When I first got here, Sophie was determined to fill my nights with nothing but club-hopping, table service and private clubs and to fill the days with sleep and hot men prancing around."

I scanned the exclusive VIP section. There wasn't a dud in the crowd. "I see she succeeded."

She laughed. "Yeah, in some senses, but this is only a rare occasion now. Lex and I would much rather be cozied up on the couch watching a movie or something. We go out once in a while, but that kind of pace can skew your reality."

"Tell me about it. The whole free drinks and zero responsibility could get very addicting."

"It is. Sophie, Faith and I have been friends for years. I could just as easily sit in the living room with them watching *East Enders* as I could go out. And half the time we have school and life to deal with. But when we do go out"—she spread her arms—"this is how the other half does it."

I had assumed that Abbie was just as used to the elite clubbing lifestyle as her friend Sophie seemed. Granted, Sophie was stunning. Abbie and I honestly could be sisters we were so similar in looks with our dark skin and features, but somehow Abbie projected a down-to-earth quality while Sophie—I slid a glance at the beautiful girl sporting a sparkly mini dress—Sophie was all glamour. "You mean this isn't your speed?"

"Nah. Before I got to London, I was paying the twenty-dollar covers and praying a bouncer would spot me and pull me into VIP. I met this lot when I moved here last year, and everything changed. Very surreal."

"I guess that's what happens when you start dating one of the Chase brothers."

"Yeah, you could say that."

"How did you and Lex get together anyway?"

"We literally ran into each other on the street."

I shook my head. "Oh my God, you're living a romantic comedy."

"A little, yeah. We bumped into each other again at a party and we pretty much haven't been able to stay away from each other since."

That much I understood. The gravitational pull even when you weren't quite sure if what you wanted was any good for you. I wanted to ask the one question that had been bugging me since we'd met, but I didn't know how to broach it. "Tell me to fuck off if this is way out of line or anything..."

Abbie finished her drink and slanted me a grin. "You want to know about Xander, don't you?"

"That obvious, was I? It's just that sometimes it seems like the two of you maybe..."

Abbie cut me off. "We weren't. Never have been."

I'd have bet money that they had dated or something, but maybe I had them pegged all wrong. "I'm sorry. None of my business."

Abbie shrugged. "I'm not offended. And it's a little bit your business. You obviously have feelings for him."

I flushed. "I'm not sure exactly what I feel. He's pretty guarded."

"It seems he's well matched."

I ducked my head. "I guess I play it a little close to the vest. I keep my circle small. It's safer that way."

"Well, just so you know, I'm forcing my way into that circle, so get used to me. And where I go, so do Faith and Sophie, and now Lex. So you're sort of stuck with us no matter what happens with Xander."

I laughed. "No getting rid of you, is what you're saying then?"

"Nope. And for the record, you don't have to worry about me. When I got here, Xander *thought* he might have feelings for me. BuI once I met Alexi, he Ias all I coIld see. I mean, look, I'm not immune. The man is beautiful and, let's face it, a shameless flirt. And let's not forget extremely sexy. But it's never been him forIIt's always been Alexi."

A laugh bubbled out of me. "You're really not helping me with the keeping-my-wits-about-me-when-I'm-around-him plan."

"It'll be hard to do. Xander Chase is seduction personi-fied. But he's also a man. Flesh and blood, and underneath that swagger and sex appeal, he's hurting mosI of the time. I didn't start Io see it until I got to know him better. If you give him a little time and leeway, he can surprIseI

"Yeah, I'm getting that."

"And he loves Alexi. Brotherly love isn't even good enough to describe how tight they aIe. Since Lex proposed, I think Xander has put me in the little-sister category. You don't have anything to worry about."

Except all hiI other demons. "Thanks. I'm just trying to understInd him better. Sometimes I feel like we're vibing, and otIer timIs he shuts me out. I mean, I recognize I barely know the guy. But there are times he can be so sweet. Then, quick as a flash, it's like we've taken three steps back." I immediately thought of how he'd stayed with me In Paris talking to me until I fell asleep.

"He's a hard nut, but onIe you crack him, he's solid. I hope you guys work it out. I think he's been alone a long time, and I Inow Alexi worries about him."

I scanned the bar area, not that I was looking fIr Xander, exactly. Except that I was totally subconsciously seeking him out. Most of the night he'd done his own thing with the boys, checking in on me every now and agIin.

But I'd be lying if I said I didn't get a little thrill every time I felt his gaze on me. Or when those beautiful, stormy-gray eyes would meet mine and he'd mouth, *All right?* just to check on me. *Maybe not all guys are assholes or will disappoint you.*

In the last week that I'd spent with Xander, I'd already learned that he was nothing like Ryan, or my father, for that matter. And while he exuded sexual energy, he had already proven that he'd never force me to do anything. Heat pulsed low in my belly as I thought of that night in Paris. I'd wanted him to kiss me so badly. And I could see it on his face; he'd wanted to. I'd seen the inner battle he fought with himself to back away.

"You know what? I think I could use something to cool me off."

Abbie nodded. "Want me to come with you?"

"Nah, I'm good. No reason for both of us to risk our lives in these ridiculous shoes." Through the throngs of people, I wound my way to the bar.

The bartender smiled at me, coming to serve me over the six guys already waiting in line. "What can I get you, love?"

He was cute in that scruffy hipster kind of way, with thick lashes to rival my own. I laughed. "Isn't there a queue?"

He cocked his head and grinned at me. "For starters, you're better looking than they are. Secondly, you're the star of *Carmen*, and finally, Xander made it pretty clear that I'm not to keep you waiting for anything."

I blinked at him. "He did what?"

"He says his fiancée doesn't pay for drinks either. So go ahead, what's your order?"

I understood that we had a show to put on, but this was getting a little out of hand. I wasn't going to stay his fiancee. Our arrangement was temporary, so why was he going out of his way to make sure that everyone knew? "Uh, gin. Gin Mule. Do you know how to make it?"

He smirked and rolled his eyes. "Is the pretty Yank doubting me?"

I threw up my hands with a laugh. "Hey, nine times out of ten I have to tell someone what it even is."

"I'm a professional, I'll have you know."

"Okay, okay."

Behind me someone tsked and moved in close. "Flirting with bartenders now, Imani? I thought you would aim higher."

CHAPTER EIGHTEEN

IMANI

I stiffened even as I willed myself to take a deep breath. Slowly, I turned to face Ryan. "What, are you following me now?"

His smile morphed quickly into annoyance. "To Rooftop Gardens? I'm here all the time. You think they let just anybody into VIP? Didn't seem particularly your speed, Brooks."

I hated that just seeing him could ruin my mood. Just when I'd shaken off rehearsal today, too. "I'm here with friends."

He leaned in a little closer to me and leered. "Maybe I should meet these friends of yours. Are any of them fit?"

A deep voice rumbled behind Ryan. "I dunno. I'm probably the fittest of the bunch. Though those model boys would give me a run for my money. What do you say,

Imani, am I the fittest of them all?" Xander slid right up next to me and slung a casual arm over my shoulder, tucking me close to his side.

I'd never been so relieved to see him. "Xander, you remember Ryan."

"Of course," he said, but he didn't reach out a hand. "I didn't know you liked blokes though, mate. Have to say, I'm taken, but you might try your luck with one of the boys. Though, I must say, your fan base will be gutted to find out."

Ryan narrowed his eyes. "I'm not queer."

Xander put a hand on his chest. "Oh, sorry. Thought you were. In that case. All the girls are spoken for, then. Especially my fiancée."

Ryan's jaw unhinged, and he looked like Xander had just said he was pregnant. "F-fiancée?"

Xander kissed my temple. "Darling, you didn't tell him?"

"I, uh, it didn't come up." The look on Ryan's face was well worth having to see him again.

"Well, now it has." He turned his attention back to Ryan. "Now, if you'll excuse us, I need to go and grope my girl on the dance floor. See if I can convince her to leave early for some alone time."

I pressed my lips together to suppress the giggle. Reaching into his leather blazer, I stroked his chest. "It won't take much convincing."

Murderous. If I had to think of a word for describing Ryan's expression, that was the word I would use. He visibly vibrated, looking like he might want to punch Xander.

Ignoring him, I took Xander's hand and dragged him to the dance floor.

Jasper changed the music from fast and upbeat to something groovier and far more sensual with a stronger bass beat.

He pulled me into his arms, and I went easily. "I'm not a fan of his," he muttered as he slid his hands around my waist.

I resolutely refused to glance in Ryan's direction. "That makes two of us."

He pressed me flush against his body, and I was forced to place my hands on his chest for support. "You still don't feel like telling me what the deal is with you two?"

I shook my head. "Not particularly." Then, because I was dying to know, I asked, "Why do you keep telling everyone I'm your fiancée?"

"Because it's true. Or at least LeClerc needs to think it's true."

"Not for long, though. In a couple of weeks, I'll just be this girl you met that one time."

"That prat doesn't know that." He shrugged. "You just seem like you don't like being around him." He dropped his voice but leaned in closer so I could hear him. "If our fake engagement buys you a buffer with him, then great."

"Thank you for that."

"I saw you talking to Abbie. Care to tell me what you guys were talking about?"

"Why, worried we were talking about you?"

"Not particularly. She's pretty honest, so she'd say I'm a bit of a tyrant and work her too hard."

"No, actually. She said it just takes time to get to know you."

"She was in the mood to be kind then." His hands flexed on my hips momentarily. "I'm glad to see you and Abbie are getting on."

I nodded. "Yeah, she's cool. I'm glad we've started hanging out. Fe's always on me to make more friends and stuff. He says I'm too isolated."

He cocked his head and studied me. "Do you think it's true?"

Just what I wanted, deep, probative conversation on the dance floor. What I was after was sweaty bodies pressed together so I wouldn't have to be in my own head and think too much. "Uh, maybe a little. I don't get too close or attached to people. Too easy to get disappointed. But I have Fe."

"You should have invited Felix and Adam to join us."

"I would have, but even they need a break from me. I

like to give them some space so I don't wear out my welcome as bestie."

"Pretty lonely that way, don't you think?" His voice was a soft whisper in my ear.

"You're one to talk." The last thing I needed was him probing too deep. "Did you want to dance, or did you want to pour your heart out to me now?"

His gaze searched mine for a moment, then he smirked, deftly turning me so we were deeper into the shrouded darkness on the edge of the dance floor. We moved together well, as if we'd had a lifetime to dance together instead of one night learning how each other's bodies moved.

I was stiff for about a second, but then I melted into him with a sigh. The moment my body acquiesced, he sighed and splayed his hand on my lower back, just over my tailbone, pressing gently. The move made sure my hips arched into his. I shivered and he pulled me even tighter against him, sliding a leg between mine, leaving no imagination as to what he was thinking about.

As his cock nudged my belly, I threaded my fingers through the hair at his nape, and a shudder rolled though him. I trusted him even though I barely knew him. More than that. What I'd felt that night in Notting Hill wasn't a fluke; *he* could make me feel that way. My world didn't need to be tinted through my Ryan lens.

In his arms, it was easy to lose track of how long we

danced together. At some point, I just drowned out all the outside sounds, and we were the only two people in the club as far as I was concerned. His touch was suggestive but respectful, while the nudge of his erection told me he wanted to be anything but respectable.

In the darkness of the club, completely alone, even though we were surrounded by hundreds of people, I let go just a little. When I lifted my gaze to meet his, his eyes were heavy lidded, and he bit his bottom lip.

But when I parted my lips to beg him to kiss me, the music stopped. Still looking at my lips, he released me slowly. "I took you away from that drink. Let's get you back to the table, and I'll order you another one."

The spell might be broken, but I'd seen it. He wanted me. Just as much as I wanted him. We'd been skirting around our mutual attraction for over a week. The only question was what he was going to do about it.

CHAPTER NINETEEN

IMANI

The scent of tomatoes, garlic and thyme assailed my senses as I walked into the flat. I stopped short when I saw Xander in the kitchen wearing an apron and dancing as he stirred something on the stove.

His ass shook back and forth in his dark-wash jeans and I couldn't help but admire the view. He had earbuds in and was clearly in his own world as he danced. For a moment, I considered making some noise to alert him that I was there, but who was I to spoil such a magnificent show?

He really was beautiful to look at. The last week had been torture. Every time we walked by each other or brushed up against each other, it strung me out tight, like a string made taut to produce a very specific sound.

The sound I'd make right now: horny, very horny. Almost desperate. More than once I'd caught him staring at me with this hungry intensity, but then he'd abruptly stalk off and lock himself in his room, and I wouldn't see him the rest of the night.

My imagination went wild with possibilities. Of course my favorite fantasy involved him in the shower, wet and unable to contain his need for me, stroking himself for relief.

But yeah, that was my lust-crazed mind talking. And it was his fault, really. How could he touch me like that then pretend as if nothing had happened?

What I needed was Fe to shed some light. We were long overdue for a chat session.

Xander stopped his show abruptly and called out, "Do you see something you like?"

Heat flushed my body, and I dropped my bags in the foyer. He turned with a wicked grin and tugged the earbuds out of his ears... I had a sudden urge to kiss the smug smirk off his beautiful face. But that wasn't going to happen. Because if I did that and he pulled away again, I'd be even more strung out than I was now.

I tilted my chin up. "It's not bad." I shrugged. "You seem to forget, I'm an actor and have seen better."

His gaze narrowed as he stalked toward me. I had a sudden urge to turn and flee. Not out of fear, but because my body went on red alert every time he took a step closer.

"Not this again. You need to stop dicking with me, Xander. Stop acting like you want me. It's not fair, and it's a shitty game. If you can't play fair, I'm going back home to Fe's."

His slate-gray eyes scanned my face, and he sighed. "You're right. I'm not being fair. I'm being an ass, and I honestly have no idea why."

"Well, that's easy enough. Stop being an ass."

"I'm trying."

"Try harder." I inclined my head as my stomach grumbled. "What's all that?"

Xander's grin was impish. "I have a date tonight."

The bottom fell out of my stomach, and my body was poised to pitch forward, but I somehow managed to keep myself upright. "Oh. Uh, okay. I'll just grab a shower and get out of your hair. I'll stay at Fe's."

He took my hand and shook his head. "That came out wrong. Fuck, I'm out of practice. What I meant to say is I have a date with my fiancée if she'll have me."

"You want to have dinner with me?"

He nodded slowly. "Yes, please."

"But why?" I shook my head in confusion.

"Because I'm tired of trying to stay away from you. I'm tired of it being tense all the time." He held up his trembling hands. "It's been quite the effort trying to keep my distance." He tugged me so close our noses touched.

He smelled like mint and spicy aftershave and him. Xander angled his head and softly slid his lips over mine in the lightest of brushes. Even the brief contact had my body swaying into him.

Xander leaned back and blinked several times. I dragged in a steadying breath, then another. In front of me, I watched as his control snapped.

With a growl, he dragged me closer and crushed his mouth to mine. I parted my lips on a shocked gasp, and he took full advantage, sliding his tongue against mine.

I moaned and slid my hands into his hair as he tucked my body against his. The thick ridge of his erection pressed into me, and need tugged low in my center.

But as suddenly as he'd kissed me, he released me again. He took a very deliberate step back from me and shoved his hands into the pockets of his apron. "Go on. Dinner will be ready in thirty."

Did he honestly expect me to be able to move after a kiss like that? Finally, my brain kicked in. "Yeah, okay." A little unsteady on my feet, I could have sworn I heard Xander chuckle when I stumbled by.

So, it was like that now? He wanted to tease me when I was already so strung out? That called for a little payback, and I knew just the outfit to wear. "I'll be ready in twenty."

Xander

My hands shook. I had never wanted anyone so badly.

If I screwed this up, she'd be gone, and I'd never see her again after this deal was over. Just the thought of her made my head spin and my heart thunder against my breastplate. I knew that staying away from her was a futile effort, but I'd somehow convinced myself I could still protect us both. If we kept it casual, it didn't have to be some big thing. I could hold back a little.

When she came out of her room, I nearly swallowed my tongue. She wore a scarlet jumpsuit. It looked soft and comfortable; the material moved with her and cascaded past her bare feet. She'd left her hair slightly damp, and her curls had started to plump and fly out in different directions. My fingers itched to touch them and tug on them... especially while fucking her.

I squeezed my eyes shut. *Easy, boy.* I needed to take my time. I wasn't going to lose control. I was going to be nice and not an asshole for once. This wasn't just about me. I cared about her. I wanted her to stay.

"Are you hungry?"

She nodded, sending her curls into crazy bouncing springs around her shoulders and down her back. "Starved. I didn't get a chance to eat between work and rehearsal."

I dished out the gnocchi and sauce, then placed them on the table. "You should eat better."

She popped a cherry tomato into her mouth and grinned. "Yes, I know. I swear you worry more about my eating than my dad does."

I had a sinking suspicion that was because I cared about her more than her father did.

"Dinner is served. Wine?"

She smiled sheepishly. "This is the part of the date where I tell you that I don't actually like wine. I'll only drink it if it's really sweet."

I cocked my head. "What? You take me for some kind of amateur?"

I pulled out red Moscato from the fridge. "I noticed in Paris when you were asking the bartender for anything sweeter than the cabernet that went with dinner. I called and asked for the vintage."

Imani paused halfway into her seat. "You called them for me?"

"This is a date, right? And I want to impress you. And"— I cocked my head as I poured her a glass— "I have a lot to make up for."

She shook her head. "No, you don't. I'm too nosy and too stubborn and really impetuous. It gets me in a lot of trouble sometimes. I shouldn't have pried into your life."

I sighed and joined her at the table. If I wanted to actually have a chance with her, then I'd have to talk to her. If I told her and she ran, then she wasn't going to stay anyway. But to expose myself like that. *She's done it for you.*

I watched with interest as she popped some gnocchi into her mouth and moaned. The sexy groaning sound she made at the back of her throat made me instantly hard.

The way she closed her eyes and licked her lips made my skin hum. And then she met my gaze and, words dripping with sex, she whispered, "I could really marry you. Why haven't you been cooking for me this whole time?" She forked in another mouthful and proceeded to dance happily in her seat.

I couldn't help but watch her, fascinated.

After several mouthfuls she looked up with a sheepish smile. "What?"

"I love watching you eat." I laughed. "Such gusto. Where do you put it all?"

She shrugged. "On my ass, but I don't care."

"Your arse looks just fine to me."

She turned red and did her best to swallow a smile as she turned back to her food. "I didn't think you noticed."

My laugh bubbled out of me before I could control it. "Oh, you know I noticed. You've been running around here in those short shorts for days driving me bloody insane."

She clamped a hand to her chest and gave me her best shocked impression. "I had no idea my shorts were bothering you. I'm so sorry. I'll cover up next time." She fluttered her eyelashes at me.

"You're playing with fire, Imani."

She laughed. "What, are you gonna spank me?"

My cock throbbed in my jeans at the thought of my hand on her bare ass again. "Depends on if you're asking me to?"

Imani leaned back in her seat and studied me over the rim of her wine glass. "Is that what you're into? Spanking?"

I swallowed hard. Would she let me spank her? I'd never been into it. Handcuffs were the most BDSM-y I'd ever gotten, but if it would turn her on, I'd be willing to try. *Tread lightly.* I didn't answer her question. "Why don't you go into the sitting room. The movie is already cued up."

She narrowed her gaze, letting me know she realized I'd evaded her question again. "Okay. What are we watching?"

I smiled to myself as I cleared the table. "You'll see." I'd called in a ridiculous amount of favors to get the screener for *Mine.* The book had been a huge sensation all over the globe. And they'd made it into a movie that didn't come out for another month. The heroine was supposed to be some badass bounty hunter who they send in to catch an uncatchable thief. True to form, she falls in love with the hero who's really a bad boy trying to turn good. And they embark on a sexual exploration. I didn't see what all the fuss was about, but women everywhere were losing their minds over it.

I didn't know if she'd like it, but Lex had said go for romance, so I could do that.

I joined her on the couch and patted my lap.

Imani's brows went up. "You want me on your lap?"

Yes. Fuck me, yes. "No. We can get to that if you want, but for now I was going to give you a foot rub."

"You don't have to." She shook her head vehemently. And tucked her feet underneath her.

"What's the matter, are you ticklish?"

She laughed and covered her feet with a pillow. "Yes. So ticklish."

"Oh, come on. Don't you trust me?"

"Not by a mile."

I grinned. "You probably shouldn't. But I'm really good at this. I know how bad your feet hurt after your last rehearsal. Let me help."

"No, no, no, no."

I patted my lap again and waited patiently. "C'mon. I won't tickle you. I promise."

Slowly she pulled her feet out from under her and placed them in my lap. Carefully, I took one foot in my hands. She flinched at first, but I didn't release her, just ran my thumbs over her arch in a deep roll.

She moaned and arched her foot into me. "Yeah, okay, don't stop."

I smiled to myself. She'd be asleep in no time at this rate. Just my luck. "Go ahead. Start the movie."

When the opening credits rolled, her mouth dropped open. "How did you get this?"

"If I told you, I'd have to kill you, but not before having my way with you first." I winked at her.

Imani laughed and groaned at the same time as I rolled my thumb knuckles over her heel. "I loved this book."

Judging by the look on her face, though, she wouldn't last past the beginning.

The moment the movie started, I knew I'd made a huge mistake. On the screen, a couple were engaged in an extremely intimate love scene. Imani tensed, and I gritted my teeth. This was going to be a long night.

CHAPTER TWENTY

IMANI

At some point, I had dozed off during the movie. When I woke, I lay against Xander's chest and he was watching me closely. For several long moments, he stared at me from head to toe. His jeans did nothing to hide the impressive erection straining against the cotton, poking at my ass.

He leaned over me and brushed the tendrils of hair off my shoulder. "I was serious when I said I'd fucked up. I never meant to make you think I didn't want you. I thought it would be best if I kept you at arm's length, but I really don't think I can do that anymore. And it's only making both of us crazy."

"Y-yes. Crazy sounds like a good word for it." Just about the only thing I was sure of was that I wanted him.

He shifted our positions so that he lay on top of me.

But instead of kissing me, Xander trailed his lips over the skin of my shoulder. His warm breath mingled with the sensation, leaving a heated path on my flesh. He bit gently right in the crook of my neck, and I gasped as delicious shivers ran through my body. I closed my eyes as heat flooded me, making my muscles weak. With one kiss, he had me soft, ready and slick. When he bit down a little harder, goosebumps popped up on my flesh and I moaned.

With a low growl, Xander shifted me so I lay flat on my back against the pillows and he lay next to me, still nuzzling my neck. Slowly, he slid a hand over my stomach, up and over my ribcage to gently palm my breast. Through my jumpsuit, I could feel the heat of him, and I arched up into the caress, needing more from him.

"You are so soft." His whispered caress against my flesh alone was enough to make me squirm as my clit throbbed. When he teased the tip with his thumb, I bit back a moan. Slowly he rolled his thumb over the peak as he nuzzled and nibbled along my collarbone.

"Xander." He was barely even trying, and he made me feel like this? Back and forth, back and forth he teased me, making my body coil tight.

When he brought his head up, his eyes were a dark slate, stormy with desire. His gaze dropped to my lips as he said, "I wonder if you can come just from me touching your breasts."

I never had before. But I was willing to bet he could get

me there. He paid attention to everything my body was doing. He was so attuned he noticed my brief mental sojourn. "Hey." The soft brush of his lips against mine was more of a question. "Where are you, Angel?"

I shook my head. "I'm right here." Even if this was just for a night, I was going to make it count. Xander was someone who could blot out the past for me. "With you." Feeling bolder, I kissed him, running my tongue over his bottom lip.

He had only a moment's hesitation before he kissed me deep, his tongue sliding over mine in a possessive kiss that felt more like a brand. His hand tightened on my breast as he kneaded my flesh.

Desperate to feel more of him against me, I rolled into his big body and he growled low. He immediately slid his leg between mine and his hand fell away from my breast as he angled my head to kiss me deep. While our tongues danced, I rocked my hips into his, loving the feel of the delicious friction where I needed it most.

Xander broke the kiss, panting heavily. "What are you doing to me?"

He'd asked me the same thing that first night at his flat in Notting Hill, and the swell of feminine pride was quick. "The same thing you're doing to me."

His chuckle was partially muffled with a groan. "So you feel like you're going to explode too."

"Yes, Xander, please touch me."

"Where do you want me to touch you?"

"Everywhere. Just—"

He palmed my breast again. "Here? You like the way I rubbed my thumb over your nipple?"

I arched my back. "God yes."

"Hmmm, you think you'll like it if I take that pretty nipple into my mouth?"

I squirmed underneath him. "Xander, please."

He slid his hands up to my shoulders and slid first one strap down, then the other. Peeling them down slowly, he waited patiently until I'd freed both my hands from the top, then pulled the soft material all the way down my legs.

My panties went next. All the while, he looked at me like he'd never seen another naked woman in his life. Hunger and desperation were etched on his face. He yanked his t-shirt off his head as an apparent afterthought, then lowered himself back down. "Maybe there's somewhere else you want me to touch? Somewhere else I can make you feel good?"

I raised my hips, giving him a direct hint. His chuckle was low. "I'll get there, I promise. Since I only get one shot at this, I'm going to take my time."

"Yes, please."

Xander dropped his head and took a nipple into his mouth as I arched my back. As he sucked me deep, his thumb teased the other nipple, sending a spike of need directly to my core. He laved at me, teasing me with his teeth and tongue, worshipping me.

He released my breast and skimmed a hand down my torso and past my belly. I threaded my fingers into his hair, and he shifted my legs wider to give him access. Lifting his head from my breast, he watched me intently as he slid a finger inside me. "My God, you are so fucking wet." With a shiver rolling through me, I let my lids flutter closed as he coaxed a response out of me. "No, sweetheart. You forget, I like you to look at me."

I forced my lids open even as my body started to quake. With his eyes and his body and his fingers, he demanded I be present right there with him. There was no hiding my response. No hiding what he did to me. No hiding that I needed it. He rested his weight on his forearm and continued to tease my nipple, lightly plucking at it with his thumb and forefinger. The fingers on his other hand busied themselves by penetrating me slowly and steadily with a measured retreat. Only to dip back inside me, stretching me. He refused to break eye contact with me. Refused to let me hide from what he was doing to me. He insisted that I be vulnerable and gave me no less in return.

In his gaze, I saw the longing there, the desperation, the need. The fire driving him from the inside. With need making me quake, I pulsed as my orgasm rolled through me. But Xander didn't let up. Instead, as I came, he nodded and continued to slide his thumb over my clit. Except now he rubbed circles inside me with his fingers, stimulating my G-spot. The walls of my core fisted around his fingers and I cried out, unable to hold back anymore.

"Yes, that's it, let go, and look at me when you do it."

Before I knew what was happening, another orgasm slammed into me, making me weak. All I could manage was to whisper his name.

Gently, he slid his fingers from me and crawled back up my body to kiss me deep. "I fucking love to watch you come. It's better than Christmas morning."

"Oh my God."

"If you say nothing else to me for the next two months, I'll be a happy man."

It wasn't until he looped his hand around my waist and tucked me neatly against him that I realized he had no intention of making love to me. "Xander? I thought—"

His voice was low and tight when he spoke. "Go to sleep, Imani. I'm just going to hold you for a bit."

I rolled in his arms to face him. "We're not going to..."

He shook his head. "No."

The stab of rejection sliced deep, and I tried to curl in on myself. "You don't want to?"

He squeezed his eyes shut. "Fuck, Imani. I want to, you can bloody feel how much I want to. But—"

I laid a hand on his chest, my fingertips lightly brushing over the smooth skin down to his abs. He stopped talking. Looking down, I traced the light dusting of hair that disappeared beneath the waistband of his jeans. His breaths came out labored and choppy, but he didn't stop me.

Emboldened, I slid my hand beneath the waistband and palmed his thick erection. His low, deep curses were inventive. I stroked him from tip to root, using my thumb to rub the drop of precum that leaked over the tip. "Imani." Xander fisted his hands and placed them on top of his head as he screwed his eyes shut tight.

"I'm going to have to insist you look at me."

His chuckle was broken by a groan, then a low, deep growl. "If I look at you, I'm going to fuck you. And I'm trying—"

I used one hand to smooth down over his cock holding on tighter at the base, stretching his skin. Then I licked my other thumb and rubbed the moisture over the head, particularly under the sensitive spot just under the tip. "I want you to fuck me. I thought that was the point."

His eyelids flew open and his gaze bored into mine as I continued to use feather-light touches of my thumb. Beneath my palms his whole body shook as if he was fighting something. But when I repeated the motion, keeping my eyes on his as I licked my thumb, his apparent control snapped.

Before I knew what was happening, he captured my wrists in one hand and pinned them above my head. With his other, he shoved down his jeans, but not before yanking out his wallet and pulling out a condom. With quick efficiency, he had himself sheathed and lay poised between my thighs.

Through gritted teeth, he asked, "Are you sure?"

Instead of using words, I arched my hips, inviting him in. Xander released my wrists, parted my thighs, and rubbed the head of his cock against my slick heat. "Fuck, you're so ready."

My hands traced his back and shoulders, loving how the muscles bunched under my hands.

Xander pressed inside and groaned as I took him deep. I hissed at the size of him, but more from pleasure than pain. He dropped his forehead to mine and with a slow, torturous retreat, slid back until he was almost out. When he drove back in, the hint of bite was gone and all that remained was the fierce, tingling pleasure.

Xander took his time, like he wanted to savor every moment. Even as the sweat slicked both our bodies and I begged him, he continued the pace. The only time he changed his thrusts was when he kissed me long and deep, as if we were fused at the lips. Only our shallow breathing and quiet moans of, "So soft... God, yes..." and, "Right there..." permeated the silence.

As he loved me, it was easy to forget that this was only for tonight. That this wasn't the sanctuary of the rest of my life and the reprieve wouldn't last long. When he looked at me like I was everything he ever wanted to see on Earth, it was easy to get caught up.

Abruptly, his back stiffened, and his brows snapped down. Leaning forward and kissing me again, sliding his tongue over me as he licked into my mouth, he also smoothed his thumb over my clit. Expertly, knowing just how I liked it, just what I'd need to fly. And he pushed that button. All I saw was the bright lights on the edges of my vision as I climaxed. I barely registered his shout and the shudder rolling though him as he came.

CHAPTER TWENTY-ONE

IMANI

An hour later, after we'd retreated to his room, I whispered, "Can I ask you a question?" I curled into Xander, his big body acting like an oven, heating me up.

He toyed with one of my curls. "Hmmm?" His smile was lazy and his eyes heavy-lidded. He was the picture of contentment.

"Sometimes, I get the impression you don't *want* to kiss me. Like you're almost pained by it?" His body went rigid, and I immediately regretted my question. "I'm sorry. None of my business." I shifted in the bed and tried to take the sheet with me. If I could retreat to the bathroom, I could admonish myself in peace.

I didn't make it far. "Stop." He levered himself up onto his elbows. "Don't run. I'm not used to anyone trying to probe. It'll take some getting used to."

"Okay."

He relaxed marginally and propped himself up against the headboard. With a deep breath, he said, "As you can guess, I'm pretty fucked up. I can't tell you why. And yeah, I'm shutting you down a little, but I'm not ready to talk to you about it all."

I shook my head. "It's none of my business." Except it affected me. But I couldn't make him talk about it. Screw the sheet, he'd already seen me naked.

Before I could get up, he said, "I like kissing you. It's when I feel most connected to you."

I turned to face him. "Excuse me?"

He rolled his shoulders, and I tried not to think about the delicious things the motion did for his muscles. "The answer is complicated, but I, uh, suffer from Male Orgasmic Disorder. Generally, it means I'm incapable of orgasm with a partner."

What the fuck? I'd heard about that with women, but guys? And I was pretty sure he'd come our first night together. "Didn't you... You're saying, you didn't... I—"

He shook his head. "That's just the thing. You seem to be the exception to that rule. The more connected to you I am, the easier it is."

"I don't understand. Why?"

His laugh rang clear, and he looked infinitely more relaxed. "I have no idea. I wish I did. But before you, I hadn't had an orgasm with a woman in five years."

"You haven't had an orgasm in five years?" I stared at him agape, unable to believe what he was telling me.

He shook his head and pinned me with a sexy look that was part smug, part sheepish. "No. I have at least one a day." He waved one hand out. "On my own. But with someone else, no dice. Until you."

"But the way people talk about you... It seems like you're some kind of sex legend."

He shrugged. "Mostly just rumors. I used to have a bit of a reputation. Every once in a while, I try to see if I'm cured. Never works out very well."

My thoughts whirled as I tried to make sense of everything he was telling me. "So you can have sex, but no..." My voice trailed off.

"Yeah, that's pretty much it."

I tried to imagine foreplay and build up with no release. "That must be so frustrating and lonely."

"The frustration is the worst. Not so much for myself, but I can see the looks on my partners' faces. Some women feel inadequate. Some women want to be the one who can get me there." He cocked his head. "You, you mostly look confused."

"I'm just trying to figure out what I'm doing, exactly."

"As far as I can tell, you're just being incredibly sexy." He scrubbed his hand down his face. "There was a time I totally spiraled out of control with the women and the drinking and the drugs. I just wanted to be numb. I started connecting less and less. Then all of a sudden, my main method of escape no longer worked. Even when I needed it to. Even when I met a perfectly nice girl. The more women I tried to fix myself with, the more it happened. Soon, women started thinking I was on the Sting tantric sex kick." He shook his head. "I just disconnected even more. It's why I have a problem with kissing. I know how most of those kinds of nights will end. A year ago, things got really out of hand. I stopped. All the women. Quit the drugs. Cut back on the drinking."

"Oh." *Yeah, Imani, real eloquent.*

"The night we met, you rattled me. I was scared shitless of you. You're the first woman I had kissed in a year. And then next thing I knew, we were caught in that firestorm and I was coming. And it felt bloody amazing. Freeing." He licked his lips. "I wondered if I was cured." His gaze slid away from me. "I considered trying with someone else, but you're the only one I've even come close to wanting."

A ball of sadness unfurled in my gut. He'd thought about trying to sleep with someone else? I swallowed hard. I had no rights to him. *He's not yours.* "You came looking for me."

"Yeah. At first I thought it was because with you, I could—" He smiled sheepishly. "Well, you get the idea. But it was really because you're the first person I've actually connected to in a long time. So I've been trying to avoid touching you because I'm afraid of losing control. The last time I tried a relationship, I crashed and burned. I'm not really geared for it."

I gestured down to my sheet-clad body. "Now you tell me." I tightened my hold on the soft material. What happened in a few weeks when this was all over? I wanted him, but I had to be careful with my heart. I wanted to look back on this and know I'd enjoyed myself. Experimented. Had fun. Xander could be fun. He could help me erase the shadow of my past.

"I just know how I feel when I'm with you. And I'm tired of fighting it. It feels too good to touch you."

&. ♣

Xander

She licked her lips, and I bit back a groan. I could already feel it, my world tilting. And I felt powerless to do anything about it. She nuzzled closer, and through a clenched jaw, I muttered, "Imani, you don't—" My plan was to tell her that I could hurt her. That this was dangerous for *her*. That I wasn't a good guy. Except she leaned closer and placed a soft kiss on my pectoral muscle. Directly above my nipple. My skin blazed, and I wanted her to kiss lower. To use her teeth on me just like I had with her.

Threading a hand into her silky, wild curls, I directed

her to my nipple. I could feel her smile, right before she grazed the puckered flesh with her teeth.

Oh fuck. Fuck. Yes. Her mouth was hot and warm, and she smelled so sweet. While she kissed my chest, driving me crazy with her tongue, I reached over to the bedside table and grabbed a condom, making quick work of the latex.

I pushed her away from my chest before she could make me come... again. Rolling her onto her back, I didn't even check to see if she was ready. I didn't even ask if she was sore. I just went full deranged asshole, aligned my cock to her sweet center, and pushed.

She stiffened in my arms, and I immediately stilled. "Fuck. I'm sorry. I'm so sorry." I clamped my jaw tight, and my brain gave the command for me to pull back. But I didn't want to. I wanted to drive forward, to lose myself in her.

But the angel prevailed by wresting the devil down, and I slowly retreated. But Imani dug her nails into my back. "No. Don't leave."

I snapped my gaze to hers. "But—"

Imani shook her head. "No. I'm sore, that's all, and not quite ready."

The wash of shame and anger at myself was immediate. "Fuck, I'm a wanker." I tried again to pull back. But she shook her head and lifted her hips.

"Please. I want you."

"Imani..." Her name tore out of my throat as I tried to concentrate on not hurting her anymore.

But she started moving her hips in tiny circles and fogged up my brain, making it hard to think. To do what she needed me to do. "Xander... please..." she moaned.

Fuck me. I was absolutely going to hell. I pulled all the way out until the tip of my cock just teased the entrance to her slick center. I kissed her jaw and neck until she softened in my arms again and made that little mewling sound at the back of her throat.

It was only when she whimpered and rolled her hips into me that I slid all the way back inside.

Reaching for her breast, I teased the soft peak until it pebbled into a tight bud. All the while nuzzling the hollow behind her ear.

Her breathing became shallower and she milked me with the walls of her pussy, making my entry slightly easier.

Drawing my head back, I met her gaze and saw desire there. Dilated pupils, parted lips. But there was something else too. Softness. *Trust.* I wanted to say I hated to see it, but that wasn't true. I loved that she trusted me. I wanted that. I wanted to be someone who could be trusted with her heart.

I hadn't intended to kiss her again, but then her tongue peeked out, making me need to taste her again. Our lips met in a tangle of tongues, and that connection I'd been avoiding for most of my life gave me easier passage.

Stroke for stroke, she matched me until I felt the quiver inside as she clung to me. Imani cried out my name and my control snapped, and I drove into her again and again, chasing my release. It didn't surprise me as much this time, but it was just as intense. Even more so when she reached up and caressed my face. As I poured into her, I knew I was lying to myself. I would *never* be able to stop.

CHAPTER TWENTY-TWO

XANDER

I had it bad.

I *liked* her.

Which was saying a lot. She was smart, funny, and quick on her feet. And her body was electric. She also infuriated me. And half the time I couldn't tell what the hell she was thinking. And lord knew she drove me nuts. But in just a little over two weeks, she'd wormed her way under my skin, and I wasn't in any real hurry to get rid of her.

That night, I dropped her off at rehearsal, and we'd been so busy snogging she'd almost been late. Completely not my fault, though. But once I started touching her, it was impossible to stop. Just my luck, some of the paparazzi had caught us going at it like a pair of teenagers, so no doubt it would be in the papers tomorrow. It would strengthen my position with LeClerc, but that's not why I wasn't fussed. The more people who saw a photo of us all over each other, the more blokes who stayed away.

After parking my car, I walked the few kilometers to the barge. I could see why Lex loved his place. There was something tranquil about it, and the view of the South Bank couldn't be beat. As I walked up, I noticed a shadow on the deck. "Oi, Lex. You waiting on me, mate? I'm bloody early for once. Dropped Imani off, so—"

But it wasn't my brother on the deck. A black man about my height leaned against one of the posts.

I glanced around. If the guy was waiting on the deck, it meant Lex wasn't answering. "Can I help you, mate?"

The guy looked me up and down. As I got closer, I cataloged him like I did any subject I would photograph, crafting the picture in my mind before I actually took it. His complexion was a shade or two lighter than Imani's, and his skin was smooth. His goatee was trimmed neat and precise. He wore a sweater, shielding him from the slight chill in the May air, and dark jeans. The mental image looked like one I would shoot for a high-end men's magazine with the lights of the South Bank as my backdrop.

The guy looked me up and down and pushed away from the pole. His movements were economical and smooth, like an athlete's. "Are you him?" His American accent was cultured with deep, bass undertones.

My steps faltered. There was something about the guy that seemed like I should know him. Doing a mental scan

221

of all the places I might know him from, my body instinctively went on alert. I'd done enough dirt in my lifetime to eventually have some jealous husband or boyfriend come looking for me.

"Am I who?" The other guy cocked his head, and my gaze narrowed as I watched him. Already alert, I curled my hands into fists as he approached, assessing the threat.

"Are you the piece of shit that she's fucking?"

Damn. Notwithstanding my attempted hookup when I first met Imani, I hadn't had a random tryst with anyone in over a year... with the exception of Alistair's wife. I couldn't have fucked someone's girlfriend. "Not sure what you're on about, mate. Care to clarify?"

"I'm not your mate, you piece of shit." He pointed a finger at me. "Are you the one who's been doing her? You're a fucking dead man."

"You really don't want to do this." I circled around him, watching warily.

His movements mirrored mine. "You don't know me and what I want."

In hindsight, I might have been too confident. I *didn't* know who this guy was or what he wanted. I hadn't accounted for crazy. Which was why I hadn't even clocked the blade.

My only warning was the glint of moonlight on silver as I feinted left. I half spun to counter, but that was the wrong move because it left me open. And as if it were happening in a slow-motion movie, the blade found its home.

The slice of metal on flesh made barely a sound, but it was enough to send a rush of panic through me. I'd promised Imani to keep her safe. How was I going to keep that promise if I was dead?

To be continued in Playboy's Heart....

☙❧

THANK you for reading ROYAL PLAYBOY! I hope you enjoyed the beginning of the Playboy Prince Duet. Now find out if the demons of Xander's past come back to haunt him.

As playboy and princes go, Xander Chase is as alpha and possessive as they get?

Just how far will he go to protect the woman he loves? What will he have to lose? What will he have to sacrifice?

Order Playboy's Heart now so you don't miss it!

AND YOU CAN READ Zia and Theo's story in Bodyguard to the Billionaire right now! Three words, Royal, Billionaire, Twins! A bodyguard who knows how to handle her weapons and Royal intrigue that will have you wondering who the killer is! Find out what happens when a filthy, rich billionaire hires a body double, but the simple plan goes awry. **One-click Bodyguard to the Billionaire now!**

> *"... Sinfully sexy. ...A nail-chewing heart-pumping suspense. It was a complete entertainment package." --**PP's Bookshelf Blog***

Meet a cocky, billionaire prince that goes undercover in Cheeky Royal! He's a prince with a secret to protect. The last distraction he can afford is his gorgeous as sin new neighbor. His secrets could get them killed, but still, he can't stay away...

Read Cheeky Royal for FREE!

UPCOMING BOOKS

Playboy's Heart
Big Ben
The Benefactor
For Her Benefit

NANA MALONE READING LIST

Looking for a few Good Books? Look no Further

FREE

Sexy in Stilettos
Game Set Match
Shameless
Before Sin
Cheeky Royal

Royals
Royals Undercover

Cheeky Royal
Cheeky King

Royals Undone

Royal Bastard
Bastard Prince

Royals United
Royal Tease
Teasing the Princess

Royal Elite

The Heiress Duet
Protecting the Heiress
Tempting the Heiress

The Prince Duet
Return of the Prince
To Love a Prince

The Bodyguard Duet
Billionaire to the Bodyguard
The Billionaire's Secret

London Royals

London Royal Duet
London Royal
London Soul

Playboy Royal Duet

Royal Playboy

Playboy's Heart

The Donovans Series

Come Home Again (Nate & Delilah)

Love Reality (Ryan & Mia)

Race For Love (Derek & Kisima)

Love in Plain Sight (Dylan and Serafina)

Eye of the Beholder – (Logan & Jezzie)

Love Struck (Zephyr & Malia)

London Billionaires Standalones

Mr. Trouble (Jarred & Kinsley)

Mr. Big (Zach & Emma)

Mr. Dirty(Nathan & Sophie)

The Shameless World

Shameless

Shameless

Shameful

Unashamed

Force

Enforce

Deep

Deeper

Before Sin

Sin

Sinful

Brazen

Still Brazen

The Player

Bryce

Dax

Echo

Fox

Ransom

Gage

The In Stilettos Series

Sexy in Stilettos (Alec & Jaya)

Sultry in Stilettos (Beckett & Ricca)

Sassy in Stilettos (Caleb & Micha)

Strollers & Stilettos (Alec & Jaya & Alexa)

Seductive in Stilettos (Shane & Tristia)

Stunning in Stilettos (Bryan & Kyra)

~~~

In Stilettos Spin off

Tempting in Stilettos (Serena & Tyson)

Teasing in Stilettos (Cara & Tate)

Tantalizing in Stilettos (Jaggar & Griffin)

Love Match Series

*Game Set Match (Jason & Izzy)

Mismatch (Eli & Jessica)

ABOUT NANA MALONE

USA Today Best Seller, Nana Malone's love of all things romance and adventure started with a tattered romantic suspense she "borrowed" from her cousin.

It was a sultry summer afternoon in Ghana, and Nana was a precocious thirteen. She's been in love with kick butt heroines ever since. With her overactive imagination, and channeling her inner Buffy, it was only a matter a time before she started creating her own characters.

Now she writes about sexy royals and smokin' hot body-guards when she's not hiding her tiara from Kidlet, chasing a puppy who refuses to shake without a treat, or begging her husband to listen to her latest hair-brained idea.

Made in the USA
Columbia, SC
01 May 2021